Ferd. Gustav Oehme

The Homoeopathic Domestic Physician

Anatiposi

Ferd. Gustav Oehme

The Homoeopathic Domestic Physician

Reprint of the original.

1st Edition 2023 | ISBN: 978-3-38230-047-0

Anatiposi Verlag is an imprint of Outlook Verlagsgesellschaft mbH.

Verlag (Publisher): Outlook Verlag GmbH, Zeilweg 44, 60439 Frankfurt, Deutschland
Vertretungsberechtigt (Authorized to represent): E. Roepke, Zeilweg 44, 60439 Frankfurt, Deutschland
Druck (Print): Books on Demand GmbH, In de Tarpen 42, 22848 Norderstedt, Deutschland

THE

Homœopathic Domestic Physician

AND

TRAVELLER'S MEDICAL COMPANION:

CONTAINING PLAIN INSTRUCTIONS
FOR CURING DISEASES, INCLUDING THOSE OF FEMALES
AND CHILDREN, BY HOMŒOPATHIC REMEDIES.

BY

DR. FERD. GUSTAV ŒHME,

Late Homœopathic Physician in Dresden, Saxony. Author of the supplement to "Rueckert's Klinische Erfahrungen (practical experiences) in der Homœopathie," and American correspondent for "Hirschel's Zeitschrift fuer Homœopathische Klinik."

CONCORD:
EDSON C. EASTMAN.
BOSTON: OTIS CLAPP.
1859.

PREFACE.

Although there is no defficiency in the number of "*Domestic Physicians*," yet I have written one more, hoping that the entirely new internal arrangement will render its use easier and more successful, and the size prove more convenient, than others.

To those who prefer larger works, I would say, that very much may be written in a small book by avoiding all unnecessary words and explanations.

Latin medical terms have been avoided as far as possible.

THE AUTHOR.

Concord, N. H.

NOTE. Purchasers of *Domestic Physicians* should always make themselves generally acquainted with the contents of their books, as soon as possible, in order to be somewhat prepared in case of sudden sickness.

CONTENTS.

FIRST PART.

INTRODUCTION.

General remarks about Homœopathy and the Homœopathic treatment of diseases.

SECOND PART.

TREATMENT OF DISEASES.

THIRD PART.

THE REMEDIES

Recommended in this book, are the following:

1. *Aconitum* napellus, (monk's hood).
2. *Arnica* montana.
3. *Arsenicum* album.
4. *Belladona* (deadly night-shade).
5. *Bryonia* alba.
6. *Calcarea* carbonica, (lime).
7. *Cantharides* (spanish flies).
8. *Carbo* vegetabilis, (charcoal).
9. *Chamomilla* vulgaris.
10. *China*, (Peruvian bark).
11. *Cina*.
12. *Cocculus* indicus.
13. *Coffea* arabica.
14. *Colocynthis*.
15. *Digitalis* purpurea, (fox glove).
16. *Hepar* sulphuris.
17. *Ignatia*.
18. *Ipecacuanha*.
19. *Mercurius* solubilis Hahnemanni.
20. *Nux* vomica, (vomit nut).
21. *Opium*.
22. *Phosphorus*.
23. *Phosphori acidum*.
24. *Pulsatilla* pratensis.
25. *Rhus* toxicodendron, (poison ivy).
26. *Silicea*, (quartz).
27. *Spongia* marina tosta, (sponge).
28. *Sulphur*.
29. *Tartarus emeticus*.
30. *Veratrum* album.

PART FIRST.

GENERAL REMARKS ABOUT HOMŒOPATHY AND THE HOMŒOPATHIC TREATMENT OF DISEASES.

CHAPTER I.

The Founder of Homœopathy and its Principles.

Samuel Christian Fridrich Hahnemann, the founder of Homœopathy, was born in Meissen, Saxony, the 10th of April, 1755, and died in Paris, the 2nd of July, 1843. After having practised medicine for several years, he became so firmly convinced, not only of the uselessness, but even of the injuriousness of the allopathic method, that he threw up his entire practice, supporting himself by the publication of chemical books and the translation of old medical works. In the course of these studies he found this remark: "*Veratrum* cures cholera, but also causes a very similar disease in those well persons who eat of it;" also, "*China* cures intermittent fever, but also causes a very similar malady in well persons." He found many like remarks here and there in several works. Considering the old practice of treating frozen limbs with cold water, and burns with heat, he at length came to the conclusion, that probably *every disease, or, in general, all complex symptoms could be cured by that medicine, whose characteristic effects upon the system, when in a state of health, most resemble the characteristic symptoms of the disease—like cures like; similia similibus.*

Assisted by his friends and afterwards by his pupils, he immediately made extended experiments to prove the correctness of this opinion, which had already in previous years been found by eminent medical writers to be a strange, perplexing truth. After years of manifold and convincing experiments he proclaimed this truth openly, and was the first, who, proving and defending the proposition, announced it as *a law of nature.* At first he gave the medicine selected according to this principle, but in large doses, as usual in allopathic practice. He soon found, however, by experience, that very small quantities of medicine, prepared in a particular way, not only operated better, but the disease was cured without leaving behind the injurious effects of large doses. He was also the first to ask the very important question : "HOW MUCH MEDICINE IS NECESSARY TO PRODUCE A CURE?" While the Allopathists ask, "how much can the patient bear?" i. e., without *immediate* danger to life, careless about engendering other and especially chronic complaints. Thus, for example, in the allopathic practice, Mercury is often given so long and in such daily increased doses, that salivation results, or the teeth become loose and other symptoms of the Mercury appear. Other medicines are used in like manner.

To those who doubt the effect of small doses of medicine, I would say, as there are poisonous exhalations in the atmosphere, which, in small quantities that can not be tested, produce diseases, such as cholera, yellow fever, etc., why may we not suppose, that a remedy, producing a cure, can be prescribed also of infinitessimal quantities. Similar analogies can be found in chemistry, physics, etc. Thus, a very little yeast only is required to raise a large quantity of dough, the same being true in other kinds of fermentation. The effect of light in daguerreotyping is another instance of great results from slight causes.

The 3d principle of Homœopathy is, *never* to give *mixed remedies*, but always only *one* at a time, while the Allopathists administer two or more mixed together.

CHAPTER II.

The Homœopathic Therapeutics.

The principle, "*similia similibus*," opened the way for the establishment of a new and *natural* system of Therapeutics. It was now the task to accurately determine the effects of medicines by the accounts of accidental poisonings and by the provings of the medicines on healthy persons, in order to employ them in the treatment of like diseases. From these provings, it appeared, that every remedy affected not only one organ and produced one malady, but more or less affected *every* organ and therefore produced *several* diseases. Therefore in this method of therapeutics by ascertaining the name of a disease, one never finds the medicine as in allopathy, as EVERY *medicine may be useful in* EVERY *disease, if the characteristic symptoms of both agree. The* NAME *of a disease,* NOT THE SYMPTOMS, *is therefore of* NO *value in the* HOMŒOPATHIC *treatment.* However strange this at first may appear, yet there is really in it a new proof of the naturalness of the homœopathic method. For as there is often some variation from sound health which it would be difficult or utterly impossible to distinguish by any accurate *name*, so there appear groups of symptoms in the remedies, which can not be accurately distinguished by *one name.* There are frequently diseases, especially chronic, to which apply not merely one, but many names. Under the symptoms of the remedies you find exactly the same. Finally, the names of all diseases are artificial. Physicians, that they may more easily understand each other, have agreed to call certain combinations of symptoms by certain names, but every acute observer will daily make the observation, that all cases of one disease, for instance typhoid fever, differ from one another in many symptoms, although all have similarity enough to be called by *one* name. I will explain this by an example: there are many kinds of trees; men have agreed to call every species by a certain name; take for instance the Maple. It has certain peculiarities commonly recognized under this head, but you scarcely find two, which resemble each other exactly. The same is the case with diseases. The *homœopathic treatment* takes *each* case *for one of its own*, therefore the medicine is to be selected with reference to the symptoms, which a certain case has *in common* with others of the same kind, but *also and especially in regard to those, which it has of its own*, as an *individual* case. This the Allopathic neglects.

It results from this, that the study of Homœopathy is much more difficult, than that of Allopathy, for the diagnosis of a disease is generally found with ease, while the estimation of *every single* symptom and the selection of the proper medicine is often very difficult.

In the third part of this book, the effects or operations of the medicines are given, or in other words, the symptoms of those diseases are mentioned, for which the medicine is to be used. *This is done as completely as is necessary for all but physicians.* Complete therapeutics for non-professionals would be an impossibility.

CHAPTER III.

The use of the book.

The design of this book is two-fold: 1. To give instructions to the people, how diseases which are *frequently recurring, yet simple in their treatment*, may be treated homœopathically. 2. To direct *early attention* to cases of a more dangerous character and to render *timely* assistance. For this reason acute diseases (those of short standing or feverish character) are particularly mentioned, and only a few chronic ones, (those of long standing,) as treatment of the latter is often very difficult, even for a physician. The number of diseases and remedies is therefore much greater than here enumerated; and even of the diseases mentioned, there are more forms than here noticed, although of less frequent occurrence. But for the design of this work, those noticed are fully sufficient for domestic use.

For greater convenience and system, all diseases are arranged according to the organs. Following each, are mentioned its remedies, which are enumerated as nearly as possible according to the frequency of their use. Where it was practicable, the chief symptoms of every remedy, as an indication to its selection, are mentioned. But never select the medicine on account of these, but first read what has been said in the 3d part of this book, regarding it and the corresponding remedies, as these indications are only slight hints and by no means a sufficient guide to the selection; it will frequently happen that one will choose a different remedy after a careful reading of the 3d part.

In selecting the remedy according to its operations, mentioned in the 3d part, consider first the general remarks concerning it; then the symptoms of the diseased organ; finally, those of the other organs. Females may always notice what is mentioned under sexual system, even in those cases, where the sexual system is not affected. The nearer the general and special symptoms of the remedy and disease agree, the better the remedy is adapted, and the sooner it will cure. Therefore the more careful one is, the speedier will be the recovery.

The best method of selecting medicine is, to write down the symptoms of the disease, not in continuous writing, but one under another. In doing this, avoid all *conjectural* symptoms, or *names of diseases*, as bilious, liver complaint, dyspepsia, humor, etc., but write what is really seen or felt. It is easier choosing the medicine, when you see the symptoms written, than when you have them only in mind.

Do not be prevented from selecting a remedy, although you find more symptoms under it, than your disease shows, but take it, if you find there all, or at least, the most prominent. Or in other words, *a remedy is right, if the character of the disease and the remedy are in the same proportion to each other, as the sketch to the finished picture.*

The homœopathic treatment of any disease, whether of a dangerous or trivial nature, is not very easy, it being sometimes more difficult to cure tooth- or head-ache, than an inflammation of the lungs. Therefore do not be discouraged, if upon the first trial, your treatment does not result in the expected success, as everything requires experience.

CHAPTER IV.

The administration of medicine.

Form and quantity. Dissolve ten or twelve globules in about one-half a cup-full of water, stirring it well, and take of it with a teaspoon, or take three or four globules in your mouth. In cases of vomiting, it is advisable to give tho medicine without water.

Frequency. If dangerous diseases, as cholera, croup, hemorrhage, etc., appear very violently, give the remedy from every half to one-fourth of an hour, even every five minutes. In *acute* diseases it will generally be sufficient to give the medicine from every two to three hours; in *chronic*, once or twice a day, or every other day.

The administration and quantity of medicine for children does not differ from that of grown persons.

Time. Unless there is necessity of immediate need of medicine, it should not be given until about two hours after eating; also, not later than fifteen minutes before.

Selection of a NEW *remedy*, when the former one proves unsuccessful. The longer a disease naturally lasts, the more slowly the improvement and healing will appear; the more rapidly a disease proceeds, the sooner improvement and recovery may be expected. As the frequency of taking medicine depends on the same conditions, it is best, in regard to the selection of *another* medicine, to observe the following rules: 1. If the disease is *not* increased, give the same medicine at least four times, before you give another; 2. If the disease increases, give the first medicine at least twice, before you give a second. In general observe this rule: *change the medicine rather too seldom than too often.*

Remedies in alternation. Although it is decidedly better to use *only* ONE *remedy*, yet there are sometimes cases, where it proves successful, to give two, but never more, in alternation; that is, use one remedy at the 1st, 3d, 5th, etc., time of taking medicine, and the other at the 2d, 4th, 6th, etc., time. The following is a list of the remedies, which *may* generally be used in alternation:

Acon., in alternation with almost every medicine.
Arnic., " " Acon., Bell., Sulph.
Arsen., " " Acon., Chin., N. vom., Sulph.

Bell., in alternation with Acon., Bryon., Hep., Merc., Sulph.
Bryon., " " Acon., Bell., N. vom., Rhus, Sulph.
Calc., " " Hep., Merc., Puls., Silic., Sulph.
Canth., " " Acon., Bell.
Carb., " " Ars., Chin., Sulph.
Cham., " " Acon.
Chin., " " Ars., Carb., Hep., N. vom., Acid. phosph., Puls., Sulph.
Coff., " " Acon., Bell.
Digit., " " Acon., Bell.
Hep., " " Calc., Chin., Merc., Silic., Spong., Sulph.
Merc., " " Acon., Bell., Hep., Silic., Sulph.
N. vom., " " Ars., Bryon., Chin., Op., Sulph.
Opium, " " Nux vom., Sulph.
Puls., " " Acon., Calc., Chin., Sulph.
Rhus, " " Acon., Bryon., Sulph.
Silic., " " Calc., Hep., Merc., Sulph.
Spong., " " Acon., Hep.
Sulph., " " almost every medicine.
Tart. emet., " Acon., Ipec., Sulph.

The strength of the medicine is destroyed by exposure to sunlight or heat.

CHAPTER V.

The homœopathic diet.

This is a general rule: every patient should have simple, unseasoned food and drinks, avoiding all such, as he knows to be injurious to himself. Starving is not at all required, as many think. Affections of the mind are to be avoided, also severe mental and bodily exercise.

Acute, or fever patients. The temperature of the room must not be too warm, and the air should be kept pure by frequent ventilation. Perspiration should by no means be produced, neither suppressed or interrupted, if it appears of itself. The face, neck, and hands may be carefully sponged with lukewarm water once a day or oftener.

Food of these patients. Fresh water, sometimes with sugar and the juice of raspberries or oranges; tea of cocoa-shells or of linden-flowers, toast-water, crust coffee, oatmeal gruel, (particularly in cases of diarrhœa) or similar dishes and drinks; white bread with butter, sometimes a small piece of cake made of eggs, flour, milk and sugar. If there is no diarrhœa small quantities of strawberries, raspberries, apples not too sour, oranges, grapes, boiled, fresh or dried fruits.

Chronic and convalescent fever-patients. Suitable mental and bodily exercise; if possible, daily walking or riding in the open air.

Food of these patients. All spirituous drinks (except wine or beer in some cases,) also coffee, and tea, are strictly forbidden, but milk, butter-milk, whey, chocolate, (not seasoned,) cocoa, and the other drinks, mentioned above, are allowed. All sour, and seasoned food or drinks, all acrid plants, as onions, celery, parsley, succory, etc., are also forbidden; also, all kinds of fish without scales, as eels, etc.; *fat* meat, particularly pork (except lean, smoked *raw* ham;) also, all *fat* food; finally the meat of water-fowls, as geese, etc.

Except the above mentioned food, all other is allowed. The best meat for patients is that of boiled doves, roasted wild game, (lean,) boiled beef, and chickens.

All kinds of scented waters, washes, tooth powder, (except burned bread, or charcoal—sour milk being the best for cleaning teeth,) pomade, (except pure beef marrow, oil of almond, alone or mixed with spermaceti,) incense-powder, etc., are forbidden.

Warm and cold baths with or without soap, (unscented,) applications of warm poultices, (not medicinal,) or of cold and warm water are allowed; but not the use of salves (except *pure* lard or oil,) medicinal washes, plasters, etc. Mustard poultices are allowed in very few cases only.

All kinds of bleeding are strictly forbidden.

Cold or warm water injections, with or without soap, (unscented,) or of milk or pure sweet oil, are allowed.

After every meal take moderate and proper exercise, and drink in the course of every day at least a pint of fresh water.

PART SECOND.

TREATMENT OF DISEASES.

CHAPTER I.

Diseases of the Brain, Nervous System and Mind.

1. *Inflammation of the Brain.*

This disease is mentioned here, not to explain the treatment, but only to correct erroneous opinions, to enumerate its symptoms, and to draw seasonable attention to the danger.

Inflammation of the brain occurs much less frequently than is generally believed. Grown persons are seldom attacked. Children suffer from it more frequently, but by far not so often as appearances indicate. They have symptoms of affection of the brain in almost all severe diseases, and the younger they are, the oftener and more severely, on account of the great irritability of their nervous system.

The common and remarkable symptoms of this disease are the following: violent fever, dry heat, redness of the face, giddiness, headache, unconsciousness, *somnolency*, delirium, *squinting*, *convulsions*, *snoring*, vomiting, constipation, etc. With children, particularly, the *head is thrown back, with a continual motion, as if to bury itself in the pillow, the hands sometimes grasping the back part of the head.*

Acon., in the beginning, fever. *Bell.*, chief remedy. *Bryon.*—*Arnic.*, external injury.

Sun-stroke requires a similar treatment.

2. *Sleeplessness; sleepiness; drowsiness.*

The most common causes of *sleeplessness* are rising too late in the morning, too much mental application, partaking of coffee, tea or other stimulating drinks, eating too much or too late, mental emotions, passions, etc.

Acon., or *Op.*, mental emotions. *Coff.*, chief remedy in most cases, excitement. *Ignat.*, grief, homesickness, sleeplessness attended by itching. *N. vom.*, mental application, coffee. *Opium*, with aged persons. *Puls.*, eating too late.

Bell., sleepiness, but impossibility of falling asleep. *Sulph.*, *Arsen.*

Sleepiness or drowsiness of long standing is always an important symptom and requires the treatment of a homœopathic physician. *Opium*, *Tart. em.*, *Bell.*

3. *Headache.*

The treatment of this complaint is often very difficult, because it is produced by a great variety of causes and has accompanying symptoms as numerous and varied.

Bellad., rushing of blood to the head, flushed face. *Pulsat.*, with pale, chilly persons. *Nux*, costiveness, sedentary life, close mental application. *Chin.*, loss of blood, nursing. *Coff.*, great excitement, nervousness. *Arnic.*, after external injury. *Acon.*, much fever. *Calc.*, or *Sulph.*, especially in chronic cases. *Bryon.*, pain in the forehead. *Ipecac.*, nausea, vomiting. *Chamom.*, *Ignat.*, *Coccu.*, *Colycinth.*, *Arsen.*, *Opium*, *Mercurius.*

Almost all acute diseases are preceded or attended by headache, therefore do not neglect the other symptoms, but endeavor to distinguish the disease at its outset, and read what is said in the proper chapter. Compare *general illness.*

In reference to diet see the preceding chapter.

4. *Giddiness.*

Giddiness is like headache, seldom a disease of itself, but a symptom, and may like headache be found in almost every sickness. Therefore, if an acute disease is coming on, or the patient is yet suffering from it, see what is said under the proper head.

Bellad., rushing of blood to the head, flushed face. *Pulsat.*, pale, chilly persons. *Nux*, costiveness, sedentary life, close mental application. *Chin.*, loss of blood, nursing. *Arnic.*, after external injury. *Acon.*, much fever. *Coccul.*, swinging, rocking in a ship, riding in a carriage. *Ipecac.*, nausea, vomiting. *Coff.*, *Calc.*, *Op.*, *Ignat.*, *Phos.*, *Bryon.*

The treatment of giddiness does not differ from that of headache. Patients inclined to either, should abstain from coffee, wine, tea, late hours, mental application, affections of the mind, etc.

5. *Apoplexy and Palsy.*

Always dangerous diseases. Remove all the clothes and lay the patient as gently as possible, in an easy position, with the head high.

Apoplexy. *Arnica*, in most cases. *Bell.*, or *Op.*, unconsciousness, red face. *Nux*, etc.

Palsy. *Arnic.*, *Bell.*, *Rhus.*, *Cocc.*, *Nux*, *Bryon.*, *Veratr.*, *Canth.*, *Puls.*, *Sulph.*, etc.

No bleeding. Apply a mustard poultice to the calves of the legs in cases of apoplexy.

6. *Fainting fit.*

A common fainting fit, particularly with sensitive females, is without any danger and does not require medicine. Loosen the clothes, lay the patient in an easy position, open the windows, rub the feet and hands, and sprinkle cold water in the face. Do not use *too much* strong smelling fluids. In cases where the application of medicine is necessary, select one from the following:

Op., or *Coff.*, terror, fear. *Puls.*, hysteric or bloodless females. *Chin.*, during or after weakening diseases, loss of blood. nursing, etc. *Acon.*, or *Veratr.*, caused by violent pain. *Ipecac.*, caused by the sight of blood. *Bellad.*, chronic diseases of the heart or lungs. *Arn.*, external injury. *Coff*, sudden joy.

Vomiting after fainting fits is not dangerous. The sleep after these should not be disturbed.

7. *Nightmare.*

This complaint is often caused by an improper

manner of living. Eat little in the evening, take light food, avoid coffee, tea, etc.; take daily exercise in the open air, and use cold baths. *Op.*, *Nux*, *Ign.*, *Sulph.*

8. *St. Vitus' Dance.*

It is an involuntary, constant movement of the limbs and body, except during sleep. The patient is conscious but unable to avoid moving. *Ignat.*, *Bell.*, *Nux*, *Sulph.*, etc.

9. *Epilepsy.*

Take care that the patient does not injure himself during the spells and that his clothes are loose.—*Ignat.*, *Bell.*, *Op.*, *Calc.*, *Sulph.*, etc.

10. *Convulsions, Fits, Cramps of the calves of the Legs, Lock-Jaw.*

Convulsions are in most cases not a disease of themselves, but symptoms, and may be caused by mental emotions, pregnancy, worms, etc. It is better to consult a homœopathic physician, although they are not often of immediate danger, except when they appear in the last stages of pregnancy or during the delivery and confinement, in severe diseases, or when they attack infants.

Bell., almost chief remedy. *Cham.* or *Ipecac.*

diarrhœa, particularly with infants. *Nux*, lock-jaw. *Op.*, or *Ign.*, after terror, fear. *Chin.*, during weakening diseases, chronic diarrhœa, etc. *Coff.*, irritable persons. *Cina.*, worms. *Verat.*, *Acon.*

Cramps of the calves of the Legs.—*Sulph.*, or *Veratr.*

Lock-Jaw after external injury, is always dangerous. *Bell.*, *Ign.*, *Veratr.*

11. *Face-ache, or facial neuralgia.*

Periodical, one-sided pains, mostly in the whole half of the face and head. They usually commence suddenly, last from several minutes to some days, stop suddenly and return at varied intervals. The pain is often very violent. *Nux*, *Bell.*, *Puls.*, *Chin.*, *Merc.*, *Coloc.*, *Silic.*, *Acon.*, *Coff.*

12. *Hypochondriasis.*

This unnatural disposition of the mind is caused by different diseases and therefore difficult to be cured by a non-professional. Compare, what is said under *diseases of the stomach*, *costiveness and flatulency*. *Nux*, *Sulph.*, *Arsen.*, etc.

If caused by self-pollution or excess of sexual intercourse, *Chin.*, *Ac. phosphor.*, *Calc.*, *Nux*, *Sulph.*

13. *Some anomalous nervous affections.*

They are very seldom diseases of themselves, but usually symptoms of others, either visible or latent; therefore they cannot always be entirely removed without curing the disease..

Nervousness. *Coff.*, in most cases. *Chin.*, after weakening diseases, loss of blood, etc. *Bryon.*

Inclination to weep.—*Puls.*

Peevishness.—*Nux.*

Great agony of mind.—*Arsen.*, *Veratr.*

Liability to sudden fright.—*Bell.*, chief remedy. *Ign.*, *Coff.*

If the recommended medicine should prove unsuccessful, give it alternately with *Sulph.*

14. *Mental Emotions.*

Excessive affections of the mind have a very great influence upon the whole system. You may prevent or remove their dangerous effect by giving one of the following remedies:

Acon., terror accompanied by vexation. *Op.*, fright, terror. *Ignat.*, home-sickness, grief, sorrow, mortification. *Bryon.*, *Nux*, or *Cham.*, vexation, anger. *Coff.*, sudden joy, sensitiveness and irritability.

If a real disease has been caused, for instance, diarrhœa, compare what is said under the proper head.

CHAPTER II.

Diseases of the Eyes.

1. *Inflammations of the eyes.*

In the following, only those kinds of inflammations are mentioned, which may generally be treated by a non-professional. For this reason, those caused by gonorrhœa and syphilis and those of the internal parts of the eye are omitted, on account of their extreme dangerousness.

(*a.*) *The catarrhal inflammation.*

The prominent symptoms are redness, painfulness, lacrymation, dread of light, sometimes fever, headache, etc.

Acon., in the beginning. *Bellad.*, dread of light. *Merc.*, *Hep.*, *Nux*, *Puls.*

(*b*) *Inflammation caused by Scrofula*, occurs

very often, particularly with children, between their 2d and 12th years, who suffer from other symptoms of this disease; also with grown persons, who have suffered from it in their childhood. This kind of inflammation is very liable to relapses. The chief symptoms are redness, very great dread of light, swelling and adhering of the eyelids, films, spots or ulcers on the cornea, etc.

Acon., in the beginning. *Bellad.*, dread of light. *Merc.*, *Hep.*, *Sulph.*, chief remedies. *Rhus*, *Calc.*, *Ars.*

If the disease is chronic, *Hep.*, *Sulph.* *Merc.*, or *Calc.*, once or twice a day, or every other day.

The application of cold water is usually injurious in this kind of inflammation, but to wash the eyes with lukewarm water, or to apply warm bags filled with bran, wet or dry, proves very useful.

(c) *Inflammation of the eyes of the new born*, commonly caused by dust, external injury or bright light. The symptoms are dread of light, redness, swelling, secretion of a thick mucous. The healing is impossible without strict avoidance of noxious influences. The eyes should be carefully cleansed from the mucous by bathing with a soft, wet sponge. The best way is, to hold the head of the child above a basin and pour lukewarm water slowly on the root of the nose; the running water, closing and opening of the eye-lids will remove the mucous and pus in the most tender manner. It should be done as often as necessary.

Acon., in the beginning, then *Ignat.*, chief remedy; if ineffectual, *Hep.*, *Merc.*, *Sulph.*

2. Weakness, dimness of Sight.

This may be a symptom of very different diseases of the eyes; therefore if there is no relief from one of the following remedies within one or two weeks, it will be advisable to consult a physician.

Chin., after weakening diseases, loss of blood, etc. *Calc.*, with aged persons. *Arnic.*, after external injury.

3. Sty on the Eye-lid.

Puls., chief remedy. *Calc.*, induration. *Sulph.*, liability to it. A warm poultice of bread and milk, left on during the night, is often of great service.

4. Foreign substances in the Eyes.

It is often very difficult to remove foreign substances. The best way is this: dip the whole face in a basin, half full of water, and open and shut the eyes very often. If this proves ineffectual, take both ends of a thick hair, with the thumb and forefinger, so that it forms a bow, push the same slowly under the upper eyelid, as far as possible, but without touching the eyes with the fingers and then draw it back. *Arn.*, *Acon.*

It is very useful to bathe them often in cold water, particularly when the air is filled with much dust.

CHAPTER III.

DISEASES OF THE EARS.

1. Mumps, or inflammation of the gland of the ear.

A swelling of the great salivary gland lying under and in front of the ear, particularly with children. This disease is attended by redness and pain of the affected part, fever, pain, and dullness of the head. The pain extends into the neck and ear in severe cases. Festering is very seldom.

Acon., fever; *Merc.*, chief remedy. *Bellad.*, affection of the brain. *Pulsat.*, metastasis to the testicles. *Hep.*, *Silic.*, or *Calc.*, festering.

2. Inflammation of the ear.

This inflammation attacks usually the auditory passage and is attended by very violent pains, heat, and redness of the affected part.

Acon., fever; *Puls.*, chief remedy. *Bellad.*, affection of the brain. *Merc.*, *Hep.*, or *Silic.*, festering.

3. Ear-ache.

Pain, often very violent, in the auditory passage without any visible inflammation. The pain is caused usually by taking cold. *Puls.*, *Bellad.*, *Merc.*, *Cham.*, *Nux.*

Apply nothing externally, except a small piece of cotton.

4. Running from the ears.

Scrofulous children suffer from this disease frequently. Often the consequence of measles, small-pox, scarlet fever, or inflammation of the ear. Sometimes difficult to be cured. *Merc.*, *Sulph.*, *Silic.*, *Calc.*, *Hep.*, *Puls.*, *Bell.*

Make every day one or two injections, either

of warm water, soap and water, or milk, but of nothing else; put also a piece of cotton in the ear.

5. Buzzing in the Ears and Hardness of Hearing.

The causes of these diseases may be very different. If the auditory passage is obstructed by dried wax or foreign substances, remove it tenderly by an ear-pick or hair pin, after having made, if necessary, some injections of warm water and soap. If the membrane of the drum or other parts of the ear are destroyed, there is no help. *Puls.*, *Bell.*, *Sulph.*, *Merc.*, *Phosph.*, *Calc.*, *Silic.*

CHAPTER IV.

DISEASES OF THE NOSE.

1. Cold, Catarrh.

Acon., in the beginning, then *Merc.*, chief remedy, running, soreness. *Nux*, stoppage, dryness. *Puls.*, loss of appetite, *Ars.*, *Cham.*, *Bryon.*, *Tart. emet*, *Sulph.* (Explanation of catarrh see under *Calcarea.*)

2. Swelling of the nose and eruptions.

With children, suffering from chronic cold, it happens often, that the nose and upper lip are swollen and bloated. *Calc.*, *Hep.*, *Merc.*, *Sulph.*, *Silic.*

Swelling caused by external injury, *Arn.*

Very red and painful swelling, *Bell.*, *Bryon.*, *Merc.*

If the tip of the nose is red, or there are red spots, *Carb.*, *Rhus*, *Acid. phosph.*

If there are scabs or scurfs in the nose or on the nostrils, *Tart. emet.*, *Silic.*

Scabs on the tip of the nose, *Carb.*

"Coppernose," caused by drinking spirituous drinks, *Ars.*, *Carb.*, *Bell.*, *Rhus.*

3. Stoppage of the nose and polypus.

Dry stoppage of the nose with infants, *Nux*; externally the application of sweet oil. Stoppage caused by swelling of the mucous membrane, particularly with scrofulous children, *Calc.*, *Silic.*, *Hep.*, *Puls.* It proves useful to draw cold water into the nose every morning.

Polypus of the nose, *Calc.*, to be given for a long time every other day, or twice a week; *Puls.*, *Hep.*, *Silic.*

4. Bleeding from the nose.

If the bleeding is not considerable, particularly in acute diseases, use nothing.

Arn., external injury, but also in other cases. *Acon.*, or *Bell.*, general excitement, flushed face. *Nux*, wine, coffee. *Puls.*, catarrh, sneezing. *Cina.*, or *Merc.*, worms. *Silic.*

Bleeding from the nose with females, whose terms are slight or have ceased, *Puls.*, *Bell.*, *Bryon.*

Very violent bleeding and danger of bleeding to death, *Ipec.*, *Cin.*, *Merc.* ; *Chin.*, debilitated persons.

Bleeding often recurring from slight causes, *Carb.*, *Phosph.*, *Sulph.*

CHAPTER V.

DISEASES OF THE MOUTH.

1. Apthæ, thrush, sore mouth.

Infants frequently suffer from this contagious disease, adult persons seldom. There are little white spots, like mould or film, on the mucous membrane of the mouth and tongue. The disease is caused, usually, by uncleanliness or by sour stomach. Care should be taken regarding cleanliness, and nursing paps entirely avoided. *Merc.*, *Sulph.* A weak solution of *Borax* frequently proves successful; dissolve a piece of the size of a pea in a tumbler of water and give the child a small teaspoonful five or six times a day.

Nursing sore mouth, see Diseases of Females, 5, *b*, 15.

2. Scurvy in the mouth, stomacace.

There are little ulcers on the mucous membrane of the mouth, particularly on the gum, which are very painful, causing putrid odor and much salivation. The gum becomes spongy, swollen, looses its natural color, separates itself from the teeth, and bleeds easily. This disease is attended by disorder of the stomach and bowels, by swelling of the adjacent salivary glands, and slow fever. *Merc.*, chief remedy; *Carb.*

3. Inflammation of the tongue.

The tongue is swollen, sometimes three or four fold, and looks purple. If the whole tongue is inflamed, festering is very seldom, but not, if there is only one part inflamed.

Acon., then *Merc.*, sometimes *Canth.*; *Arn.*, external injury.

4. Infected breath.

Usually caused by food remaining and putrifying in a hollow tooth or between the teeth.—*Cleanliness.* If produced by any disorder of the stomach or bowels, see what is said under the proper head. If caused by ulcers of the mouth, throat, or nose, *Merc.*

5. Salivation.

If produced by disordered stomach, see what is said under the proper head. If caused by diseases of the salivary glands, teeth, or mucous membrane of the mouth, *Merc.*, but if by having taken too much Mercury, *Hep.*

6. Change of taste and coated tongue.

Usually caused by derangement of the stomach or bowels. See therefore what is there said. A *bitter* taste is very commonly, but falsely, taken for a sure sign of biliousness, and a *sour* taste, of a sour stomach, whereas they are only symptoms of a disordered digestion in general. But sour eructations or raising of sour food are signs of a sour stomach; and raising or vomiting of a bitter, greenish phlegm may indicate a disease of the liver or bile.

7. Toothache.

Toothache is not always caused by decayed teeth. It is known by experience, that hollow teeth sometimes do not cause pain, even when so perfectly decayed as to fall out; and that teeth, not at all hollow, sometimes are very painful. Therefore it is not necessary to have these teeth extracted immediately. It is often very difficult to select the right medicine, because symptoms, and often apparently very trifling ones, must be considered.

Acon., or *Coff.*, pain almost insufferable. *Bell.*, rushing of blood to the head. *Puls.*, pale persons. *Chin.*, nursing females, debilitated persons. *Merc.*, decayed teeth. *Arn.*, *Cham.*, *Nux*, *Rhus*, *Calc.*, *Silic.*

There is nothing better to preserve the teeth, than cleansing the mouth with lukewarm water after eating and especially before going to bed; also rubbing of the teeth and gums with a brush dipped in sour milk, once a day.

8. Dentition, teething.

The appearance of the first teeth is attended

usually with pain, inflammation of the gum, and some other complaints, which, if neglected, may endanger life, although too many diseases are frequently supposed to be caused by dentition.

When a child is about six or seven months old, the teeth make their appearance in the following order: the two middle lower front teeth, the upper ones, the two lateral lower front teeth, the two upper ones, then the jaw teeth in the same manner, etc. Before the teeth cut through, the gum usually becomes broader, swollen and whitish, the mouth is hot, the child gets uneasy and drools, puts the fingers or other things in the mouth and bites. A great variety of symptoms sometimes make their appearance.

Coff., excitement. *Acon.*, fever. *Cham.* diarrhœa, uneasiness. *Calc.*, chief remedy. *Bell.*, affection of the brain, convulsions. *Ign.*, convulsions.

CHAPTER VI.

DISEASES OF THE THROAT AND CHEST.

1. INFLAMMATION OF THE THROAT, SORE THROAT, QUINSY.

There is redness and swelling of the palate,

uvula and tonsils with pain and difficult swallowing. Festering is seldom. In all diseases of the mouth and throat the patient should be examined; let him open the mouth and the tongue be pressed down with a spoon.

Bell., in the beginning, or sometimes *Acon.*, if much inflammation, fever, then *Merc.*, chief remedies. *Cham.*, *Nux*, *Hep.*

2. Hoarseness and Aphony.

Compare what is said under *cough* " and *cold.*" Sometimes it is a symptom of chronic diseases of the throat or lungs, such as consumption, etc., and then it can not often be entirely removed.

Bell., in the beginning, or sometimes *Acon.*, then *Merc.*, chief remedies in acute cases. *Carb.*, or *Phosph.*, in chronic cases. *Hep.*, liability to it. *Cham.*, *Puls.*, *Sulph.*

3. Croup.

This disease of the throat is always a dangerous one, but can be easily cured by homœopathic remedies, in most cases. Children, almost exclusively, till their eighth or ninth year, particularly scrofulous ones, are attacked by this disease, which appears mostly in cold and moist weather with a dry, cold wind.

Children are usually troubled with a slight, sometimes hollow cough and hoarseness a few days before the appearance of croup, but sometimes these premonitory symptoms do not appear. The patient awakes suddenly in the first part of the night with a dry, hollow, rough, barking, hoarse cough, attended by great uneasiness, distress, hoarseness, pain in the throat, fever, short or difficult breathing. The child usually falls asleep after this, but is awakened soon by a second, more violent spell. The cough is then rougher, hollower, hoarser, like the hoarse bark of a dog.

Every single coughing is followed by a short, hissing or whistling inspiration. The voice is hoarse, rough and soundless. Between the spells there is a whistling or sawing sound in the windpipe at each breathing. Sometimes the cough is attended by unsuccessful efforts to retch or vomit something out of the windpipe, but usually there is no discharge of mucous. In the second stage, at times, mucous, and afterwards, small or large pieces of solid and sometimes pipelike masses, are retched out. The difficulty of breathing increases more and more, the patient sits up with evident anxiety, holds fast to something, grasps the throat, and bends the head backwards. If medicine is not used, the spells of suffocation become more frequent and violent; it is easily noticed, that an impediment opposes the passage of the air in the throat; the face becomes bloated and bluish, and is covered with cold perspiration, the limbs become cold, the pulse imperceptible and the patient suffocates, showing the greatest agony.

Sometimes the disease disappears of itself towards morning; the patient, during the day, is a little hoarse and feverish, coughs at times, and seems almost well, but in the night there comes on a new attack, more violent than before.

This is almost the only disease in which the patient should be woke to take medicine.

Spong., chief remedy, given every two hours, or if necessary, every hour or half hour, or even every five minutes. If there is much fever and heat, give *Spong.* and *Acon.* alternately, every two hours or oftener. *Hep.*, chief remedy next to *Spong.*, is especially to be considered, when there is *much hoarseness* and *much loose, tough* phlegm in the throat, causing heaving and vomiting; also in cases of long standing, or when the patient is liable to relapses. *Phosph.*, very malignant cases, when croup has caused diseases of the lungs.

The medicine which has proved beneficial, should be given one day longer, than the disease lasts, once in three or four hours, or at least as long as the cough has the peculiar croup tone.

When during a spell there is much inclination to retch or vomit, or when much mucous seems to be in the windpipe or throat, it is beneficial to give the patient some draught of warm water, with or without sugar; it alleviates the raising of mucous. It is also beneficial in this disease to apply a warm poultice to the throat, but take care, that it does not get cold.

No bleeding, no emetics.

4. Cough, acute and chronic catarrh.

Cough may be a symptom either of severer diseases of the throat or lungs, such as pneumonia, consumption, etc., (in these cases compare the following with what is said under the proper head,) or of a simple catarrh, often attended by a cold in the head.

Remedies, particularly used in acute *catarrh*, are the following:

1. Especially in the *beginning*, when the cough is *dry*,—*Acon.*, much inflammation, fever. *Bell.*, spasmodic, convulsive cough. *Nux*, tickling in the throat. *Cham.*, *Bryon.*, *Ign.*, *Cina*, *Ipec.*, *Veratr.*

2. Especially in the *second* stage, when the cough is *loose,—Puls., Ipec., Merc., Tart. emet.*

Remedies particularly used in CHRONIC *catarrh*, *—Sulph., Phosph., Ars., Carb., Calc., Acid. phosph.*

But this division is not without exceptions, being only a slight hint for the selection of medicine.

Chronic coughs cannot always be entirely removed, but may be frequently much relieved.

Explanation of Catarrh see under *Calcarea.*

5. Influenza.

Influenza is an epidemic cold or catarrh of the nose, throat and lungs, but attended by more general weakness, irritability and fever, than a simple catarrh. Compare what is said under "*cold*" and "*cough.*"*—Merc., Acon., Bell., Nux, Phosph.,* etc.

6. Hooping cough.

Usually children, seldom grown persons, are attacked by this disease, which consists in a catarrhal inflammation of the lungs and ramification of the windpipe. The disease is infectious, and often epidemic. Hooping cough commences usually with a common cough or cold, but this begins soon to come on by spells, and consists of several short, quick, successive whoops, after which, suddenly, follows a long and deep inspiration with a loud, whistling, shrilling or shrieking sound. Such an attack lasts one or several minutes and returns in proportion to the violence of the disease, as from one to five times in an hour or once a day. Very often there seems to be no sign of the disease in the intervals. If the spells are violent, they announce themselves by agitation and great uneasiness, the patients then hold fast to something, bend their head forward, and begin to cough, sometimes so rapidly, that they have scarcely time to recover their breath; they seem almost to suffocate, and become purple in their face. Usually the spell is terminated by raising mucous or by retching or vomiting of mucous or food. There is more or less fever. The disease lasts from three to twelve weeks and changes sometimes to chronic diseases of the lungs.

Acon., much fever. *Bell.*, chief remedy, spasmodic, convulsive cough. *Veratr.*, much vomiting, great uneasiness. *Ipecac.*, choking, suffocating cough. *Cina*, stiffness of the body, worms. Sometimes the other medicines recommended under *cough*, are useful.

The patient should constantly be in equal temperature during the whole disease. He may be allowed to walk out (if the disease is not very violent and the weather warm and calm) and to take simple and nourishing, but easily digested food. When there is great liability to vomit, he may eat often, but only a little at a time.

7. Inflammation of the lungs, pneumony.

This disease commences often with severe chills, followed by heat. There are pressing or stinging pains, particularly when breathing and coughing ; difficult, quick, short respiration ; cough, in the beginning dry, then with a tough, bloody expectoration, looking like iron-rust ; quick, full pulse ; giddiness, headache, thirst, red urine ; the patient lies on the back (not on one side); weakness. Inflammation of the lungs is usually attended by partial pleurisy. The diagnosis of both diseases can be made certain only by a well learned physician.

Acon., in the beginning, fever, then *Sulph.*, chief remedies.—*Arnic.*, after external injury. After *Acon.*, sometimes *Bry.*, stinging pain, or *Bell.*, affection of the brain. Instead of *Sulph.*, sometimes *Phosph.*, *Tart. emet.*, *Merc.*

8. Consumption, tuberculosis.

To be treated only by a homœopathic physician. Compare what is said under *catarrh, hoarseness, spitting of blood, inflammation of the lungs, and pleurisy. Sulph., Phosph., Merc., Calc., Bell., Arn., Bryon., Chin., Puls., Ars., Silic., Acid. phosph.*

9. Spitting of blood, with or without cough.

Blood or bloody mucous is thrown up by coughing or "hawking," from the lungs. Observe, if it may not come from the gum, nose or throat. It is in most cases a symptom of other diseases, particularly of inflammation of the lungs or of consumption. Therefore compare what is said there. Sometimes caused by suppressed terms, and in these cases compare what is said under the proper head.

Arnica, almost chief remedy. *Bell., Acon., Phosph., Chin., Bry., Puls.*

10. Hemorrhage from the lungs.

Often a symptom of diseases of the lungs, particularly of consumption, in some cases caused by suppressed terms. It is sometimes attended by vomiting or retching. The patient should not be allowed to speak or move, and should lie with the chest erect, in rather a cold room.

Acon., full, hard pulse or fever, then *Ipecac.*, or *Arn.*

When the patient looses so much blood, that there is danger of bleeding to death, dissolve a spoonful of table salt in half a cup of water and let the patient drink it. After that, give the proper medicine either every fourth, or half, or one or two hours. Cloth dipped in cold water, may be applied to the chest, and warm cloths to the legs, or a mustard poultice to the calves of the legs.

When the attack has entirely passed and the patient is left very weak, give some doses of *China*; also if he faints during the bleeding.

11. Short, difficult breathing; asthma.

This complaint usually appears in periodic spells and is often a symptom of diseases of the lungs or heart; compare therefore, what is said under the proper head. Sometimes not to be cured entirely.

Ars., or *Ipec.*, chief remedies. *Nux*, *Bell.*, *Veratr.*, *Coff.*, *Puls.*

12. Short, difficult breathing of children.

(Asthma Millari infantum.)

This attacks young children, and very much

resembles croup, although it is not a disease of the throat, but a nervous affection of the lungs. It appears suddenly (without any premonitory indication) like croup, but has neither the inflammatory symptoms of the throat, nor is attended by cough, unless a slight, dry, rough one. There is no symptom in the intervals. The child wakes usually from a very natural sleep with an attack of suffocation, accompanied by a sawing sound in breathing; no pain in the throat, but often a sensation as if the upper part of the chest were cramped. The child is quite well the next day and has no fever, but a new spell appears the next night, usually more violent. The death of the child by suffocation is possible.

Ipec., chief remedy. *Ars. Veratr.*, *Tart. emet.*

13. Pleurisy.

It is an inflammation of the membrane (skin) covering the outside of the lungs, lining also the inside of the chest. It is distinguished from pneumony by a more violent stinging pain, rendering motion and breathing very difficult; no cough, unless a slight, dry one. *No bloody* expectoration.

Acon., in the beginning, fever, then *Bryon.*, chief remedy. *Sulphur.* *Arn.*, external injury.

14. Inflammation of the heart.

This dangerous disease is very seldom alone, but usually attended either by pneumony, pleurisy or rheumatismus acutus. There is fever, irregular pulse, great uneasiness, pain in the region of the heart, etc. Compare what is said under *asthma, and palpitation of the heart.*

Acon., in the beginning, fever, then *Ars.*, chief remedy. *Bell.*, *Veratr.*, *Puls.*, etc.

15. Palpitation of the heart.

A frequent symptom of various diseases and in these cases cannot be entirely removed, without curing the disease.

Acon., vexation. *Cham.*, vexation, sudden joy. *Coff.*, sudden joy or terror. *Opium*, terror. *Veratr.*, fear, agony. *Ignat.*, grief, mortification, indignation. *Chin.*, nursing females. *Bell.*, flushed face. *Puls.*, pale face. *Acid. phosph.*, debilitated persons. *Ars.*, *Nux*, *Digit.*

CHAPTER VII.

DISEASES OF THE STOMACH.

1. Disordered, overloaded stomach.

This complaint is caused by faults in diet, as eating too much fruit, greasy or fat food, ice-cream, etc. If neglected, it may change into catarrh of the stomach, compare therefore, what is there said. If too much food has been taken or of too various dishes, half a cup of strong coffee without milk is the best.

Puls., fat food, fruits. *Nux*, spirituous drinks, milk, coffee, tobacco; *Ipec.*, nausea: *Bryon.*, milk; *Ars.*, fat, sour, or too cold food; *Phosph.*, too cold food; *Carb.*, spirituous drinks; *Acon.*, sweet food; *Coff.*

2. Nausea and vomiting.

Both complaints are often symptoms of other diseases, therefore compare what is said under the proper head.

Ipecac., chief remedy, overloaded stomach. *Puls.*, *Nux*, *Bryon.*, *Tart. emet.*, *Arn.*, *Chin.*, etc.

Vomiting of blood.—*Ipec.*, if insufficient, *Ars.*

3. Eructation; Heartburn; Hiccough.

Eructation.—*Bryon.*, *Nux*, *Puls.*, when bitter. *Calc.*, *Nux*, *Phosph.*, when sour. *Hep.*, *Tart. emet.*, when fetid. *Nux*, *Bell.*, in pregnancy. *Cocc.*, *Veratr.*

Heartburn. *Nux*, *Phosph.*, *Chin.*, *Calc.*

Hiccough. *Ignat.*, *Nux.*

4. Catarrh, weakness of the stomach, dyspepsy.

This diseaso may appear from different causes, viz: effects of allopathic and patent medicino, irregular habits, diseases of the heart, lungs or liver, etc. It shows the following symptoms: want of appetite, belching, pain, distress, nausea, vomiting, flatulency, coated tongue, general illness and weakness.

Nux, costiveness, sedentary habits; *Bryon.*, costiveness; *Puls.*, fat, flatulent food; *Ipec.*, or *Tart. emet.*, nausea, vomiting; *Chin.*, constant sensation of being satiated; *Calc.*, sour stomach; *Hep.*, liability to this disease. *Phosph.*, *Ars.*, *Cham.*, *Sulph.*

Explanation of Catarrh see under *Calcarea.*

5. Sea-sickness.

Compare what is said under *giddiness*, *nausea*

and *vomiting*. *Coccul.*, chief remedy. *Ignat.*, *Bell.*, *Sulph.*, *Nux.*

As much exercise as possible should be taken in all cases, or at least one should be on deck in the middle of the ship, (even in unpleasant weather) and eat frequently a small quantity of simple food, although forced. Some persons are relieved by drinking a little brandy or rum, or by putting blotting-paper, soaked in rum or brandy, on the pit of the stomach.

6. Pain in the stomach.

This complaint is frequently a symptom of other diseases, as chronic catarrh, ulcers, indurations or cancer of the stomach. Therefore some cases can be cured, others only relieved.

Nux, *Ars.*, *Bryon.*, chief remedies. *Bell.*, *Coccul.*, *Ignat.*, *Phosph.*, *Cham.*, *Carb.*, *Puls.*, *Chin.*, *Sulph.*

CHAPTER VIII.

DISEASES OF THE LIVER.

Under this chapter only jaundice is mentioned, as the diagnosis and treatment of the other diseases is too difficult, to be noticed here.

Jaundice.

This disease consists in retention and partial resorption of bile in the blood, and is usually caused by catarrh of the stomach or duodenum (first part of the intestines,) spreading over to the ducts of the bile. There is a yellow color of the skin, particularly *of the white in the eye;* urine dark; fæces of a clay-like color; no pain.

Merc., *Nux*, *Bryon.*, *Chin.*

Jaundice of the new-born. In these cases the urine is quite natural, but the fæces are dark and bilious colored. *Acon.*, chief remedy; *Merc.*, or *Cham.*, diarrhœa.

CHAPTER IX.

DISEASES OF THE BOWELS.

1. Inflammation of the bowels.

In this disease the membrane covering the outside of the intestines, also lining the inside of the abdomen, is attacked. There are violent, stinging pains in some particular, usually not very large place, increased greatly by motion and touch, so that respiration or coughing is very difficult and painful, sometimes even the weight of the bed-covering can not be borne; fever, great uneasiness and distress, distention of the abdomen, belching, nausea, costiveness. The disease, if neglected, may prove fatal by gangrene and perforation of the intestines.

Acon., in the beginning, fever, then *Bryon.* chief remedy; *Bell.*, much colic pain; *Merc.*, diarrhœa; *Ipec.*, nausea, vomiting; *Ars.*, collapsus; *Canth.*, difficult, painful discharge of water. Apply a warm poultice.

2. Griping colic.

Nux, almost chief remedy; *Coloc.*, chief remedy in violent colic; *Cham.*, especially with children. *Puls.*, *Ars.*, *Bell.*, *Merc.*, *Rhus*, *Chin.*, *Cina.*

3. Flatulency, bloated bowels.

Flatulency is usually attended by some disorder of the bowels; compare, therefore, what is said under the proper head.

Nux, *Sulph.*, chief remedies.; *Chin.*, weakness; *Carb.*, chronic flatulency. *Bryon.*, *Puls.*, *Ars.*

4. Costiveness, constipation.

If the costiveness is a symptom of an acute disease, it is always more favorable than diarrhœa, therefore do nothing against it, except the patient becomes evidently troubled by its too long duration, after five or eight days. Common costiveness is mostly caused by improper diet or manner of living, as drinking much coffee, eating more animal food than vegetable, sedentary life, etc.

Nux, *Bryon.*, *Op.*, *Sulph.*, *Chin.*, *Calc.*, and a proper style of living. *Nux*, taken at bed-time, and *Sulph.*, in the morning, will remove most cases of common costiveness. If the fæces are too hard, make an injection of warm water and soap.

It is often caused by drinking very little or no water. Everybody should drink at least two tumblers of water during the day, particularly some in the morning before breakfast. If the costiveness is very obstinate, take every morning a cold sitting bath and thoroughly sponge the whole spine. Sometimes a daily injection of cold water, continued for some time, proves useful. If you accustom yourself to an evacuation every day, at a certain hour, and do not suppress the natural call, you will be unlikely to become costive. Physic will give relief only for a short time, leaving the disease worse than before.

5. Diarrhœa.

Looseness of the bowels may be a symptom of catarrh of the intestines, commonly called diarrhœa, or a symptom of a great many diseases; in the latter cases compare what is said under the proper head; in the former, select one from the following remedies:

Ipec., nausea, vomiting; *Merc.*, greenish or bloody stools, tenesmus; *Bryon.*, taking cold; *Puls.*, fat food; *Cham.*, particularly with children; *Veratr.*, cholera-like attack; *Ars.*, fetid smelling stools; *Coloc.*, violent colic. In chronic diarrhœa, or liability to it,—*Sulph.*, *Chin.*, *Calc.*, *Acid. phosph.*, *Hep.*

Explanation of Catarrh see under *Calcarea.*

6. Dysentery.

Dysentery is an inflammation of the mucous membrane (interior skin) of the great intestine and rectum. There are very violent discharges of a slimy, membranous, bloody fluid, mostly without fæces; very violent tenesmus and pain in the anus, particularly before and after every discharge; colic, fever, want of appetite, etc.

The disease makes its appearance particularly in summer and fall, and is usually epidemic.

Acon., violent fever, then *Merc.*, tenesmus, or *Coloc.*, violent colic,—chief remedies. *Ipec.*, nausea, vomiting. *Arsen.*, fetid smelling stools. *Puls.* or *Nux*, in slighter cases.

7. Cholerine and Cholera.

(Cholera Morbus.)

Both of these are treated in one chapter, because they are only different degrees of one and the same disease, the treatment being alike.

In *cholerine* there are frequent discharges, first, of fæces, then of a bilious, or watery matter. In *cholera* there are frequent discharges like rice-water; coldness of the skin, which is not elastic but retains every impression; suppressed secretion of urine; feeble, almost imperceptible pulse, and collapse of the whole body. In both diseases are found vomiting, pain and colic in the bowels, thirst, anxiety, debility, cramps, particularly of the calves of the legs.

Veratr., chief remedy; *Ipec.*, much vomiting; *Ars.*, much thirst and collapse; *Carb.*, asphyxia, malignant cases; *Acid. phosph.*, cholerine with painless diarrhœa.

When cholera makes its appearance without

vomiting and diarrhœa, but with immediate collapse, bluish color and coldness of the skin, great uneasiness and distress, suffocation, groaning and sighing, spasm of the muscles and jaws, cold tongue and breath, dissolve a little camphor in a cup of water and give every ten minutes one tea-spoonful. The above mentioned medicines are to be given every ten or fifteen minutes, if the attack is very violent. In many cases of coldness of the body, it proves useful to rub the whole body with warm cloths. Use no herb tea.

8. Typhoid fever, typhus.

To be treated only by a homœopathic physician. The disease commences usually with headache or dulness of the head, want of appetite, general illness, costiveness or diarrhœa, pain in the bowels, little or no fever. These symptoms last often a week before the patient perceives that he is really sick, and confines himself to the house or bed. But sometimes the disease makes its appearance very rapidly. The most common symptoms are the following: headache, dulness of the head, afterwards delirium, disagreeable feeling through the whole system ; pains, particularly in the right and lower part of the abdomen, just over the thigh, increased by touch ; fever, want of appetite, costiveness the first days, then diarrhœa like thin pea soup, etc. *Bryon.*, *Rhus*, *Acid. phosph.*, *Carb.*, *Ars.*, etc.

9. Yellow fever.

This dangerous disease commences in most cases at night. The premonitory symptoms are the following: general uneasiness, weakness, want of appetite, or sometimes unnaturally increased; headache, chills, etc. After this the other symptoms appear in the following order: pain of the limbs and back; trembling, face puffed and bright red; general heat, sometimes interrupted by chills; eyes red and protruded, sometimes painful; redness of the skin, extending from the face over the neck and chest; thirst; no appetite, violent pain in the stomach; fever, respiration accelerated; great agony and despair; tossing about, trembling, spasms, delirium; vomiting in the beginning, of food, then of bile, afterwards of black matter, sometimes of blood; thin, blackish diarrhœa, urine red and scant, sometimes suppressed. After some days the redness of the skin changes into a yellow color.

Bryon., pains in all parts of the body, slight fever, sometimes tenderness over the region of the stomach. *Bell.*, affection of the brain. *Nux*, neuralgic pains in the spinal column, extending across the chest and abdomen. *Ars.*, almost chief remedy; black vomiting, great thirst, burning pain in the stomach, tenderness of the stomach, great debility. *Veratr.*, vomiting. *Canth.*, urinary complaints. In the beginning especially *Acon.* and *Bell.*, in alternation. The medicine is to be given according to the violence of the disease, i. e., from every ten minutes to every two hours.

10. PILES, HEMORRHOIDES.

Piles are tumor-like enlargements of the veins in the rectum and anus; they have a bluish or purplish color, are sometimes very painful and sensitive to the touch, and occasionally bleed. It is not a disease of itself, but in most cases a consequence of impeded circulation of blood; some cases, therefore, can be cured, others only relieved.

Nux, costiveness, and *Sulph.*, are the chief remedies. *Bell.*, or *Acon.*, inflammation, fever. *Ipec.*, danger of bleeding to death. *Calc.*, *Ars.*, *Carb.*, *Cham.*, *Canth.*, *Merc.*, *Coloc.*, *Puls.*

If there is danger of bleeding to death, apply ice or cold water.

Patients suffering from piles should avoid tea,

coffee, all stimulating drinks and food, sleeping in too warm beds, and should take every day a cold sitting bath and exercise in the open air. Compare *costiveness*.

Physic frequently causes piles and will always increase the disease.

11. Worms.

There are three different kinds of worms, viz: *ascarides*, or pin-worms, a small worm, like those of a cheese; *maw-worms*, very similar to mud-worms; *tape-worms*, a white, thin kind, about a quarter of an inch broad, consisting of many joints.

The *ascarides* live in the great intestine and rectum, particularly of children, causing often violent itching in the anus. The *maw-worm* and *tape-worm* live particularly in the small intestine; children suffer especially from the former, grown persons from the latter. The ascarides and maw-worm often cause, by a nervous reflexion, itching in the nose, liability to self-pollution, and fits.

Although the diagnosis is only certain, when worms have been seen in the fæces, yet it is to be suspected, when persons are always unwell, have a pale face, blue circles around the eyes, can not bear sweet food, fruits or roots, have sometimes want of appetite, or a ravenous or craving one, are suddenly attacked with pains in the bowels, fits, etc., which appear and disappear suddenly.

It is almost natural to have some worms, particularly with children, and a few of them are not productive of harm, but if they become numerous and cause the foregoing symptoms, give one of the following remedies:

Cin., chief remedy; *Ign.* or *Sulph.*, itching in the anus; *Acon.*, fever; *Coff.*, excitement; *Merc.*, diarrhœa; *Bell.*, affection of the brain; *Calc.*, or *Sulph.*, liability to have worms.

When common worm medicine is given to patients for the purpose of destroying or expelling worms, it will affect also the digestive organs. But as the weakness of these is the cause of the origin of the parasites, the system will be still more impaired by such medicines, although the desired effect may be produced for a short time. The immediate consequence will therefore be, more worms and the patient worse, than previous. Sometimes even death is caused by the intended remedy. On the contrary, it is a fact, that when digestion is improved by homœopathic medicine, the worms disappear of themselves.

The diet is of particular importance; it consists especially in the following; every day exercise in the open air and cold washing of the whole body; eating at certain intervals and not at all times; refraining from sweet food, too much bread, pie, cake and similar food. But eat frequently of raw or cooked roots, as carrots, parsnips, etc. In some cases injections of cold water every day.

12. Hernia, rupture.

Old ruptures of grown persons require under all circumstances a well fitted truss. A plate of lead, fixed by an elastic band (india rubber,) is the best truss for rupture of the navel of children. Carcerated or strangulated hernia require the attendance of a surgeon, but it is a fact, that the operation is easier performed and sometimes entirely unnecessary, by the administration of homœopathic medicine.

Acon., inflammation, fever; *Nux*, almost chief remedy; *Op.*, much distension of the bowels and red face; *Sulph.*, sometimes after *Nux*; *Ars.*, gangrene.

CHAPTER X.

DISEASES OF THE URINARY SYSTEM.

All these diseases are generally very dangerous, and therefore particular attention should be given to every complaint of this kind. The secretion of urine is of so great importance, that there is more danger, when a day passes without making water, than a whole week without having an evacuation of the bowels.

1. Difficult and painful discharge of water.

(Dysury and Strangury.)

Puls., almost chief remedy; *Canth.*, very painful; *Nux*, spirituous drinks; *Arn.*, external injury; *Acon.* or *Cham.*, after terror, vexation; *Bell.*, *Merc.*, *Sulph.*, *Ars.*

Bloody discharges.,—*Canth.*, or *Merc.*, chief remedies; *Acon.* or *Bell.*, fever.

2. Too frequent discharges of water.

There is frequent desire of making water, but only a little at a time. *Puls.*, *Bell.*

3. Wetting of the bed.

Puls., chief remedy; *Sulph.*, *Cin.*, *Bell.*, *Carb.*, *Hep.*

It proves very successful to bathe the whole body in cold water, particularly the spine. Sometimes it is well to make an injection of cold water in the anus every day. Patients suffering from this affection should not drink much in the evening.

CHAPTER XI.

DISEASES OF THE SEXUAL SYSTEM.

DISEASES OF MALES.

1. *Swelling of the testicles, with or without inflammation.*

Arn., external injury; *Puls.* or *Merc.*, metastasis of any disease to the testicles; *Acon.*, heat and great painfulness, fever; *Puls.* or *Nux*, swelling and painfulness of the back part of the testicles and of the seminal cord; *Spong.*, hardness and painfulness. *Bell.*, *Sulph.*

2. *Emissions.*

Emissions, at times, are almost natural and require no medicine, but recurring often, they weaken the whole system. Patients suffering from them, should avoid partaking of all stimulating food and drinks, eating much in the evening, sleeping in too warm beds and not longer than 7 hours, reading obscene books, thinking or speaking of obscene subjects, and indulging in lascivious intercourse with females. Take plenty of exercise every day, let the mind be constantly employed with some useful subject, use cold sitting baths or wash the sexual organs in cold water, once a day. Without strict observance of this advice the cure is almost impossible.

Nux, *Puls.*, *Phosph.*, *Op.*, *Canth.*, *Sulph.*

With weak, debilitated persons, or those who have practiced self-pollution, or have had too frequent sexual intercourse. *Chin.*, *Acid. phos.*, *Calc.*, *Sulph.*, *Nux*, *Puls.*

DISEASES OF FEMALES.

1. *Terms, menses, menstruation.*

(*a*) *First appearance and cessation of the terms.*

The first appearance of the terms is a sign

that a female has arrived at the age of puberty, usually between the 14th and 17th year. It is not a sufficient reason for the administration of medicine, if they appear earlier or several years later, as long as the general health does not suffer. The terms appear every four weeks and last from three to six days; the average quantity of discharge is from four to six ounces. After the 44th or 48th year they gradually cease. This period is commonly called the turn or change of life. A short time before and during the terms, the disposition of the mind is generally a little altered, also some pain is felt in the abdomen. During pregnancy the terms cease in most cases. Every deviation from this natural course, is disease, and peculiar care in reference to it, should be taken, as it may be the origin of a great number of diseases.

Females are generally very careless in respect to this important function of their sexual organs and to its irregularities. A short time before and during the terms every female should avoid dancing, riding on horseback, excitable mental emotions, all stimulating food and drinks, as coffee, tea, wine, etc. Also, improper clothing, too tightly laced dressing, and too sedentary habits, are very injurious. Those who are accustomed to cold baths, may, at this time, take lukewarm.

(b) Too tardy appearance of the first terms; the terms too late, too scant, too short, suppression of the terms.

In all these cases the treatment is alike and the medicine should be taken *in the intervals*, once every day or every other day.

When the terms become still less frequent and less in quantity, the disease is about changing to green sickness.

Puls., chief remedy; *Bell.*, or *Bryon.*, rushing of blood to the chest and head; *Calc.*, *Chin.*, *Sulph.*, *Ars.*, *Acid. phosph.*, *Phosph.*

(c) The terms, too soon, too copious, too long.

The medicine is to be used during the terms, three or four times a day, and in the intervals, once every day or every other day.

Nux, chief remedy in many cases. *Calc.*, *Bryon.*, *Bell.*, full-blooded persons, flushed face. *Arn.*, *Cham.*, *Coff.*, *Sulph.*, *Chin.*, *Ign.*

In obstinate cases try the following during the intervals; as soon as the terms have passed, take before going to bed the 1st and 3d day *Nux*; the 2d and 4th day, *Chin.*; the 5th, 9th, 13th, etc., day, *Sulph.*, and the 7th, 11th, 15th, etc., day, *Calc.*, till the terms appear again.

(d) Painful Terms.

Bell., bearing down pain; *Puls.*, pale, chilly persons; *Cocc.*, too scant terms; *Cham.*, *Coff.*, *Ign.*, *Nux.*

2. *Hemorrhage, loss of blood from the private parts.*

Always dangerous. In regard to the selection and administration of medicine there is no difference, if the hemorrhage happens either in pregnancy, delivery, confinement, or at any other period. Use the medicine, according to the violence of the bleeding, every 5, 10, 15 minutes, every ½, 1, 2 hours. Apply externally cold water or make cold injections in the vagina. The patient should lie with the hips considerably elevated, or at least the whole body should have a horizontal position.

Arn., after external injury, but also in other cases; *Ipecac.*, almost chief remedy in very violent bleeding; *Bell.*, full-blooded persons; *Puls.*, inactivity of the womb; *Chin.*, great weakness, fainting; *Cham.*, *Acon.*, *Bryon.*

3. *White sickness, whites, leucorrhœa.*

It is a secretion of mucous from the private parts, which, if neglected, may give rise to very obstinate diseases, or at least, weaken very much the whole system. *Puls.*, *Calc.*, *Sulph.*, *Merc.*, *Chin.*

4. *Green sickness, chlorosis.*

In this disease the whole system is affected, therefore it is better to consult a physician. There are found the following symptoms: pale, sometimes greenish color of the skin; pale, bloodless lips and gums, great weakness and debility; cold limbs and liability to chills; short breathing and palpitation of the heart after bodily exertion; disordered digestion; loathing of meat and warm food; irregular terms or entire disappearance; whites, headache, giddiness, depression of the mind, etc.

Puls., chief remedy in the beginning; *Calc.*, *Sulph.*, *Chin.*, *Ars.*, etc.

In this disease the diet and manner of living is of great importance,—daily exercise in the open air; simple, but nutritious and easily digested food; proper dressing; daily cold washing of the whole body; no excitable mental emotions.

5. *Pregnancy, delivery and confinement.*

Under this head only those diseases and complaints are treated, which make their appearence at this time; in regard to all others, as giddiness, nausea, vomiting, etc., see what is said under the proper head, as the treatment does not differ, if they occur at this time.

(a) General Remarks.

The natural duration of pregnancy is 40 weeks or 280 days. Although it is often impossible to fix the time of the birth, it may be reckoned from the following, viz: 1. The time of the last terms; 2. The commencement of morning sickness, generally six weeks after conception; 3. The first motion or quickening of the child, which occurs nearly at the expiration of half of the whole period.

1. *Diet and manner of living.* Every pregnant female should avoid all severe bodily exertion, as dancing, riding on horseback, lifting heavy weights, etc., all stimulating food and drinks, as coffee, tea, etc.; but have simple, nutritious, easily digested food, taking daily moderate exercise in the open air and wearing proper dress—never tight clothing. Neglect of these rules is the most common cause of hemorrhage, miscarriage, and often the origin of obstinate diseases. Those who cannot bear the usual quantity of food, may take a little at a time, but

frequently. The most of these rules should also be observed during the first six weeks after the delivery.

In spite of the strictest observance of all these, some slight complaints occur, particularly in the first pregnancy, as it is almost impossible, that such a great and important change of the female system, as caused by pregnancy, child-birth, etc., should occur without some illness.

2. *Warm baths to soften the private parts.* Females who have very narrow or inflexible private parts, particularly in the first pregnancy, may use warm sitting baths and rub the parts with lard or sweet oil, once a day for the last 4 or 6 weeks. When the delivery is coming on, take these warm sitting baths for 1, 2 or 3 hours, as often as is necessary, and make injections in the private parts, of warm water, warm milk, or warm sweet oil. Continued injections of warm water for one or two hours render the whole act of delivery easier, and support the labour very much. For this purpose the opening of the syringe must be near the womb, in order that the stream may reach it.

3. A short time before delivery the female should have a *movement of the bowels,* if not a

natural one, an injection of warm water and soap should be made.

4. The *breasts* should be kept carefully warm the last weeks of the pregnancy, particularly during the confinement; it is done best by covering the whole breast with a large, thick piece of wadding. Wash the *nipples* in alum water, once or twice a day, for the last six weeks, in order to harden them.

5. *Perspiration.* Take no sudorific medicine, neither drink tea nor use too warm bed-clothes on account of perspiration, except in case the mother should feel violent chills after the delivery, but take care, that the natural perspiration is not suppressed by taking cold.

6. *Costiveness*, for the first three or four days after the delivery, is natural, but diarrhœa always very dangerous. But if after the third or fourth day there is no movement of the bowels, make an injection of warm water and soap, and give internally *Nux.*

7. *Lochiæ* are the discharge from the private parts after the delivery, lasting about a fortnight. It is, the first days, like the discharge of menstruation and in the last days of a yellowish, whitish mucous. As long as this is bloody, the

mother should lie in bed, to prevent hemorrhage, falling of the womb or vagina. When the discharge begins to turn yellow, she may sit up, on the first day two hours, and then every succeeding day two hours longer.

8. *Nursing.* Every mother should nurse her child, if the health will admit. Her food should be nutritious, but simple, as porridge made of flour and milk. For the first two or three days the quantity should be rather limited; from the fifth day—if the secretion of milk is well established—she can have more hearty food and gradually resume her usual diet.

If the mother is unable to nurse, or the child dies, she should be allowed only a short diet, as gruel made of flour and water, until the secretion of milk has nearly ceased. The disgusting custom of nursing puppies is entirely unnecessary.

Regular hours for nursing should be observed as far as possible, as both mother and child, will derive great benefit from this habit. Give the breast from 6 o'clock in the morning till 9 or 10 o'clock at night once in two, or still better in three hours, and during night once, at 2 or 3 o'clock, lengthening the intervals during the day more and more the older the child grows. If it seems thirsty during the intervals give it one or two tea-spoonfuls of moderate cold water; it should not be put to the breast every time it cries, as this is not always a sign of hunger.

During the whole period of nursing she should not take stimulating food or drinks, as such have a very great and injurious influence over her milk, and consequently upon the child. If the mother is strong enough, the child may have only her milk for the first six weeks, but if not, it may also have other milk, once or twice a day. After the first six weeks, give the child other milk, or some suitable food, once a day. Wean it *gradually*, accustoming it to other food, so that it may be entirely weaned after six or eight months. Too long nursing weakens and debilitates the mother and is of no benefit to the child.

(b) Anomalies.

1. *Varicose veins* are a dilitation and distension of the veins, particularly on the legs. If they are very large and painful, rest, in recumbent position, is required. Wearing of a proper bandage or laced stocking proves very useful. *Sulph.*, *Puls.*, *Nux.*

2. *Bleeding* or *hemorrhage* from the private parts with pregnant females, is always dangerous,

as it is in most cases a premonitory sign of miscarriage. See what is said under *hemorrhage* or *loss of blood from the private parts.*

3. *Miscarriage* or *abortion.* This anomaly is, in most cases, preceded or attended by hemorrhage from the private parts, therefore compare, what is there said. It is always dangerous. One miscarriage produces liability to another at the same period of pregnancy, and the oftener they happen, the greater the liability is increased. Those who have had one should be very careful of their diet and manner of living in their next pregnancy and consult a physician.

4. *Labor, pains.* It is a law of nature, that labors are painful as well as the whole act of childbirth, therefore use medicine only in case of too painful or anomalous ones.

Coff. or *Cham.*, over-excitement, agitation ; *Acon.*, flushed face, fever ; *Puls.*, pains too weak ; *Bell.*, pains to painful ; *Op.*, stupor.

Use the medicine every five, ten, fifteen, or thirty minutes.

5. *Afterbirth.* Do not hasten to take off the afterbirth, if it should not appear soon after the birth. It may remain without danger from six to twelve hours.

6. *Bruising or injury of the sexual organs*: Take *Arnica*, internally, and apply externally water containing a few drops of tincture of *Arn.* Rents and wounds of these parts should be attended by a physician.

7. *Afterpains* are quite natural, if not too painful and of long standing, but if thus, give *Arn.*, in most cases suitable, or *Puls.*, after a too quick and easy birth.

8. *Retention of urine* for longer than five or six hours, is always very dangerous, *Arn.*; difficult birth, *Puls.*

9. *Coming of the milk,*—*Merc.*, almost chief remedy in delay of its appearance. *Puls.*, interruption or suppression of its secretion. *Bryon.*, suppression of milk after affections of the mind. *Acon.* or *Bell.*, fever. *Calc.*, involuntary flowing of the milk.

10. *Soreness of the nipples.* When the nipples are sore or this commences, wash them after every nursing with water, containing a few drops of tincture of *Arnica*, and also take *Arnica* internally. If it proves unsuccessful after some days, take *Rhus* or *Sulph.*

The nipples should always be washed carefully with warm water before every nursing. Do not use washes or salves.

11. *Inflammation of the breasts.* *Arn.*, after external injury; *Acon.*, fever, great painfulness and redness; *Bell.*, redness, painfulness; *Merc.*, festering; *Bryon.*, too much secretion of milk. *Phosph.*, *Hep.*, *Silic.*, *Chin.*

12. *Weaning.* Swelling, hardness, redness, and painfulness of the breasts originate sometimes at the time of weaning, *Bryon.*, *Bell.*, *Merc.* Keep the breasts warm with wadding and eat little for the first days.

13. *White swelling* is a painful, bright, whitish, red-streaked, elastic swelling of the upper thigh, caused by inflammation of the veins and lymphatic ducts. Often dangerous. *Ars.*, chief remedy.

14. *Puerperal fever* is always a *very dangerous* disease, and is caused, in most cases, by taking cold, suppression of the secretion of the milk or of the lochiæ, mental emotions or overloading of the stomach, etc. The symptoms are fever, painfulness of the abdomen, looseness of the bowels, diminution or suppression of the secretion of milk and lochiæ. *Acon.*, then *Bell.*, etc.

15. *Nursing sore mouth.* This disease, arising from general weakness caused by nursing, is

very frequent in North America, showing itself especially by cankerous ulcers in the mouth. The patient should immediately cease nursing and take simple but nourishing food. *Chin.*, *Acid. phosph.*, *Carb.*

CHAPTER XII.

TREATMENT OF CHILDREN.

In regard to all diseases and complaints, from which children suffer as well as grown persons, see what is said under the proper head, as there is no difference of treatment between these and adults.

1. Tying and cuting off the navel-string.

The navel-string must be tied carefully, about one and a half inches from the navel. This should be done, when the pulsation of the cord has ceased, or at least, when the child is completely alive, having breathed, etc. About two inches from the first ligature, towards the mother, the cord must be tied again and then cut in the middle of the two ligatures, with scissors, quite blunt. The second ligature is made, so if there should be twins, the second, unborn child may not bleed to death. If the child does not cry of itself, cause it to cry by sprinkling the chest with cold water, when in the warm bath. For a crying child makes deep inspirations and in this way, every cell of the lungs becomes dilated and the entire lung well adapted for respiration. While on the contrary the cells, if not dilated soon after the birth, remain forever in this inactive state, and, by adhering, become entirely useless for respiration.

Apparent death of the newborn, see apparent death.

2. Washing of the child.

The best way of removing the white unctious matter, covering the child, is, to rub it freely with lard, until the two substances become completely incorporated. After that, the child should be carefully washed with soap, in a warm bath.

3. Dressing of the navel.

The navel string should be carefully enveloped in a piece of linen, soaked in sweet oil. It is done best by cutting a hole in the middle of the linen, putting the cord through, and wrapping in it the string. This should be secured by the belly-band. Pulling on the cord is entirely to be avoided.

4. Elongation of the Head and Tumors on the Head.

When the head has become of an unnatural form by a long and difficult birth, do not try to give it a better one, as this would prove fatal. It disappears of itself. The same may be said of tumors on the head. If the tumor is large, apply externally linen, dipped in water containing a few drops of tincture of *Arn.* In case the tumor does not disappear, but becomes larger and soft, appearing to contain matter, give *Silic.*, four times a day, and call for a physician.

5. Swelling and Induration of the Breasts.

It is caused in most cases by pressure or improper dressing. Apply externally water, containing a few drops of *Arn.* If caused by inward diseases, give *Bell.*, particularly when there is redness of the affected part; when festering, *Hepar.*

6. Sniffles.

Infants suffer often from a kind of catarrh or

stoppage of the nose, which renders the breathing difficult, when nursing. Give *Nux*, and carefully clean the nose from the dry mucous. It proves useful to rub the nose externally with sweet oil.

7. Blisters on the body.

There are small or large blisters, filled with a light fluid, which burst and become dry, leaving a sore place or a scab. They appear all over the body, but particularly on the hands and feet, causing an itching and burning pain. *Rhus*, chief remedy; *Acon.*, fever, uneasiness; *Merc.*, festering.

8. Crying of infants.

We may here treat of the crying of infants, when there is no visible disease or complaint, as diarrhœa, sore mouth, etc.

As it is a fact, that infants, a few months old, do not cry without cause, it follows, that there must be some reason, if they cry. Notice if it proceeds from one of the following causes: whether the mother has drank tea, coffee, or taken improper food, or experienced an excitable mental emotion; whether she is well or not; if improper drinks or food have been given to the infant; if it is hurt by the clothes, by a pin or vermin; if it is hungry or needs changing; if the head lies too high, etc.

Besides all these causes, which ought to be avoided, they often cry in consequence of difficult and painful discharges of water, or in consequence of flatulency and colic pains; in the latter case there is usually distention of the abdomen, accompanied by emissions of wind; in the former, frequent discharges of very little water, accompanied with crying till the common quantity has passed. Compare *general illness*.

Cham. or *Colocynth*, flatulency, griping colic, uneasiness; *Nux*, colic, or when the mother has experienced a mental emotion, or has taken tea, coffee, spirituous drinks; *Puls.*, difficult, painful making of water; *Bell.*, starting from the sleep; *Coff.*, sleeplessness, excitement; *Acon.*, great excitement, heat, fever.

9. Inflammation of the navel.

If caused by improper treatment or external injury, *Arnic.*; if it is very red and inflamed, *Acon.* This disease turns easily to erysipelas.

Convulsions.—see what is said under *convulsions, fits.*

10. Lameness of children.

Although it does not happen with infants, yet it is too important a sympton, to be unnoticed.

Children often commence to walk lame and limp upon one leg without having any pain. There is, in most cases, inflammation of the joint of the hip. If this affection is neglected, it turns to festering and ulceration, the patient becoming lame for life.

Bell., in the beginning, then *Merc.* or *Carb.*

The patient should not be allowed to go about, but must quietly lie still.

CHAPTER XIII.

DISEASES OF THE SKIN.

1. Chicken pox and small pox, varicellæ, varioloides, variolæ.

The above mentioned diseases, which are all infectious, differ from each other only in the quantity and quality of the pustules and in the violence of the accompanying symptoms, as fever, headache, delirium, want of appetite, etc., also in the time of the duration of the disease, (one to four weeks).

The selection and administration of medicine are the same,—*Acon.*, fever; *Bell.*, affection of the brain; *Coff.*, excitement, sleeplessness; *Merc.* or *Sulph.*, chief remedies, festering; *Tart. emet.*, affection of the chest; *Ars.*, gangrene.

2. Measles.

This infectious, but usually not malignant disease, commences with fever and symptoms of cold and cough, (catarrh of the nose, eyes and lungs). The cough is dry and rough; scratching and burning in the throat. The eyes are usually affected with redness and sensitiveness to light. After some days, the eruption makes its appearance on the skin, in red, irregular and slightly elevated spots, more on the body and face than on the limbs. This is followed by a bran-like scaling of the skin, after the first or second week. Duration of the disease from one to three weeks.

Acon., fever; *Puls.*, chief remedy and preventative against this disease. *Bell.*, affection of the brain; *Sulph.*, delay of the eruption; *Merc.*, diarrhœa; *Ipec.*, *Bryon.*, *Coff.*

3. Scarlet fever.

This disease is infectious, often malignant and always dangerous. There are large red spots, more on the neck and limbs, than on the trunk, which disappear by pressure. It is preceded and attended by inflammation of the throat and palate, swelling of the tonsils and glands of the neck, difficult swallowing, affection of the brain, fever, etc. As long as the scaling of the skin lasts, much care should be taken against taking cold, as neglect of this may cause dropsy, even death. Duration of the disease from three to four weeks or more.

Acon., fever ; *Bell.*, chief and preventive medicine ; *Mecr.*, *Coff.*, *Op.*, *Sulph.*, *Ars.*, *Hep.*, *Bryon.*, *Ipec.*, *Phosph.*, *Rh.*

4. Scarlet rash, French measles.

The spots on the skin resemble either those of measles, or those of scarlet fever. If they are like those of scarlet fever, there are the other symptoms of measles, (cold and cough), and vice versa. Duration of the disease, from one to two weeks.

Acon., fever, and *Bell.*, chief remedy ; *Coff.*, uneasiness.

5. Erysipelas.

A great many different maladies are falsely called, by the people, erysipelas. The disease consists in swelling, redness, and painfulness of the affected part of the skin, frequently attended (especially in the beginning), by fever, want of appetite, nausea and other symptoms of indigestion. It makes its appearance mostly in the face, or on the head, less frequently on the feet and legs, sometimes slowly changing its place on the skin. It is not a dangerous disease of itself, unless it strikes inwardly in consequence of neglect or taking cold. If it is on the scalp, the brain is often affected. Sometimes there are blisters, filled with watery fluid, on the surface of the affected part (called *erysipelas bullosum*). Unless neglected, festering and gangrene seldom occur. Duration of the disease, eight days or more.

Bell., chief remedy ; *Rhus*, chief remedy with erysipelas bullosum ; *Acon.*, fever ; *Sulph.*

Apply externally nothing else than dry wadding.—no cold water.

Erysipelas of the newborn, a dangerous disease. It appears around the navel and is usually caused by improper treatment or injury of the navel string,—*Arn.*, then *Bell.*

6. Nettle rash.

This disease is sometimes very obstinate, but not dangerous, often caused by certain kinds of food, as strawberries, crabs, etc. It has the same appearance, as if the affection was caused by stinging nettles, disappearing sometimes suddenly and rëappearing again.

Bell., chief remedy; *Ars.*, caused by poisonous animals; *Rhus*, *Puls.*, *Bryon.*, *Sulph.*, *Nux.*

7. Itch.

There are small pimples, particularly on the inside of the arms, between the fingers, on the body, especially on the sexual organs,—never on the face. Violent itching, particularly in a warm bed at night. The disease is caused by a small mite, laying eggs, by which the disease is propagated; it is therefore infectious.

Sulph. chief remedy, sometimes *Merc.*

Bathe the whole body twice a day in warm water and soap, and rub the affected parts afterwards with alcohol and then with warm sweet oil.

8. Itching of the skin.

There is sometimes violent itching on the body without any disease of the skin, especially at night.

Ignat., *Sulph.*, *Silic.*, *Nux*, *Ars.*, *Merc.*

9. Blisters or scabs on the head, body, etc., scald head, salt rheum, etc.

All these diseases, the scientific name of which is *Eczem*, are called by various names on account of their different appearance, although they are by nature the same.

Small blisters, filled with watery fluid, originate on the inflamed skin during violent itching, burst, and dry off. The disease is either ended with this process, or proceeds in this way: (1.) the skin more or less inflamed, blisters of various stages, pustules, scales of different colors and sizes; or (2.) red and inflammed skin, which exudes a more or less colored fluid of a thin or thick consistence; or (3.) both of these forms are found at the same time. The first and third form can be changed always into the second by washing with warm water and soap. There is always itching. It depends upon the irritability of the patient and the violence of the disease, whether or not it is accompanied by fever and other complaints. The disease is not infectious, in most cases hereditary, and a sign of scrofula. Some cases are very obstinate, and, if treated improperly, last for life, while others only a short time, the greatest number from two to four weeks.

Rhus and *Sulph.*, chief remedies, often to be given alternately; *Acon.*, fever, much inflammation; *Coff.*, excitements, sleeplessness; *Bell.*, *Cham.*, *Merc.*, *Hep.*, *Silic.*, etc.

Daily exercise in the open air; no pork, no seasoned food, not much salt. Frequent washing with water and soap. No washes or salves. If the disease is on the scalp, the hair must be kept very short. Cleanliness.

10. Excoriation or soreness of the skin.

This affection attacks particularly infants, on the neck, under the arms, and between the thighs. In most cases frequent washing, careful drying and sprinkling with starch are sufficient, if not, give *Cham.*, *Merc.*, or *Sulph.*

11. Boils.

The skin becomes red, hard and painful, and a tumor rises, the highest part of which is in the centre. After some days pus, mixed with blood, escapes from the top and the pain ceases. Lancing gives speedy relief.

Arn., in the beginning; *Merc.* and *Hep.*, festering; *Bell.*, redness and painfulness; *Ars.*, malignant boils, gangrene; *Sulph.*, liability to it.

Apply nothing else than a warm poultice or warm water and soap.

12. Blisters, runrounds, whitlows on the fingers.

Runround is a blister on the finger, filled with a watery fluid, slowly changing its place, and causing a burning pain, *Hep.*

Whitlow or *felon* is an inflammation of a part of the finger, usually on one side of the nail, which changes always into festering. Often very painful.

Merc. or *Hep.*, chief remedies; *Acon.*, very much pain and inflammation; *Silic.*, affection of the bone.

Apply a warm poultice and use every two hours a bath of warm water and soap. Lancing will relieve all pain.

13. Frozen limbs and chilblains.

Frozen limbs are to be thawed by rubbing with ice water or snow. If much time has passed, before this can be done, they should be treated like chilblains, viz. *Arn.*, externally and internally; if insufficient, *Nitric acid*, twenty drops to one half cup of water, externally. Apply it with a pencil brush as often as required and let it dry; if it should smart much, rinse it with water. Close shoes are to be avoided.

14. Burns and scalds.

As limbs, when first frozen, are to be treated with cold water or snow, so burned or scalded limbs, with warm water. The best way is, to dip cloth of 12 or 16 folds in water, considerably warmer than bloodheat and apply it *immediately* to the injured part, allowing it to remain, *as long as the pain lasts.* The wet linen or cotton should be covered with a dry cloth in order to prevent its cooling. At first the pain is increased, but after a short while it entirely ceases, when healing will very soon take place. If too much time has elapsed, after the accident, before applying warm water, use cotton or fine shavings of new soap spread over cloth, or any indifferent substance, to cover the part from the air.

Acon., fever or much inflammation; *Canth.* or *Ars.*, burning pain; *Sulph.* or *Merc.*, festering; *Ignat.*, excitement, uneasiness; *Coff.*, excitement, sleeplessness.

15. Ulcers, open sores.

Their origin has various causes, which should be considered in the treatment.

Sulph., *Merc.*, *Hep.*, *Silic.*, *Ars.*, *Carb.*, *Rhus*, *Bell.*

Carefully cleanse the ulcer with lukewarm water, without pulling off parts of scabs, etc., and put on a piece of clean batting, sufficiently large to cover the sore, upon that a piece of flannel, and upon that again a large piece of wadding; secure all these by a bandage. To be dressed as often as necessary, every day or other day.

CHAPTER XIV.

DISEASES OF OTHER ORGANS AND GENERAL DISEASES.

1. Lame back, pain in the back.

They are symptoms of very different, mostly dangerous diseases, therefore consult a physician.

If the *spina* itself, or one part of it, is painful, especially from external pressure, it is a symptom of different diseases of this organ. Always dangerous.

If the pain is *between the shoulders* or a little lower, it is in most cases, a symptom of consumption.—*Bryon.*, *Bell.*, *Sulph.*

If the pain is on both or one side of the spine, *in the region of the last ribs*, it may be a symptom of a disease of the kidneys, as inflammation, etc. ; in such cases other urinary symptoms usually appear,—*Bell.*, *Canth.*, etc.

If the pain is *between the small of the back and the anus* it is generally a symptom either of the piles, (*Nux*, *Sulph.*, etc.), or of the periodical sickness, (*Nux*, *Cham.*, *Sulph.*, etc).

If it is a symptom of *rheumatism* of the muscles of the back,—*Arn.*, *Bryon.*, *Bell.*, *Rhus*, etc.

If caused by external injury, *Arn.* Compare what is said under the proper head.

2. Losing of the hair.

Calc., *Chin.*, *Acid. phosph.*

3. External injury, contusion, concussion, bruises, sprains, wounds, overlifting, dislocations, fractures, etc., after operations, etc., foreign substances.

Compare *headache* and *giddiness*, *foreign substances in the eyes* and *herniæ*.

It is impossible to give full directions for the treatment of all these different affections, especially as some of them require invariably the attendance of a surgeon, but still some advice may be useful for the treatment of slighter cases, or till medical aid can be procured for severer ones.

Use in *every one* of the above mentioned affections *Arnica* internally and apply externally cloth, folded several times and dipped in *Arnica*-water (ten or fifteen drops to a cup of water). This prevents, as far as possible, the swelling and aids the healing.

Severe injuries always require rest of the affected part, either by wearing a bandage, or by *general* rest.

Foreign substances must be removed as soon as possible,—*Arn.* or *Acon.*, the latter in much inflammation; *Hep.*, festering.

Wounds, if not clean, are to be washed in cold water and the edges kept together by a proper bandage, as sticking plaster.

When blood spirts out of arteries, the bleeding may be stopped by pressing a piece of cloth on the wound or by compression of the artery a little above the affected part. Compare *bleeding, hemorrhage.*

When fever makes its appearance, give also *Arn.*; if it is violent, *Acon.*, or both, alternately; when festering comes on, *Hep.* or *Merc.*

When a nervous affection, as numbness or prickling, remains in the affected part after the healing, or when much time has elapsed after the injury and *Arnica* proved unsuccessful, give *Rhus*.

Convulsions and lock-jaw are dangerous symptoms.

No salves, plasters, etc.

4. General illness with or without fever.

It often happens, that a person is attacked by general illness, with or without fever, and is unable to designate his complaints with certainty by any particular name, and consequently knows not how to look for its appropriate treatment. This general illness may or may not be the commencement of some disease.

If the complaints are caused by excitable mental emotions or by poisonous substances, see what is said under the proper head; if caused by improper food, see *disordered* or *overloaded stomach*; wearing wet clothes, use *Rhus*; taking cold, or in general, if there is fever, heat or chills, want of appetite, dullness of the head, *Acon.*; but when the brain is particularly affected, or there is starting in the sleep, *Bell.*; if caused by dissipation, *Nux*, or *Ars.*; loss of rest, *Chin.;* debility after severe diseases, loss of blood, sexual excess, or other weakening causes, *Chin.* or *Acid. phosph.;* over-exertion, too fatiguing exercise, etc., *Arn.;* if general illness comes on, when an epidemic disease prevails, take the chief remedy for that disease, (if typhoid fever, *Bryon.* or *Rhus*). Explanation of fever see under *Aconit.*

5. General weakness and debility.

It is either a premonitory symptom of an approaching disease, (compare general illness,) or the consequence of having suffered from sickness, loss of blood, broken sleep, or other weakening accidents,—in these cases see what is said under *Chin.* or *Acid. phosph.;*—if the consequence of too fatiguing exercise, *Arn.*

6. Bleeding, hemorrhage.

Place the part, from which the blood flows, as high as possible, apply externally cold water, ice or vinegar, or a mixture of these. Compare *bleeding from the nose, from the lungs, from the private parts.*

Arn., after external injury or operations, also in other cases; *Acon.*, full, hard pulse, fever; *Ipec.*, chief remedy in very violent bleeding;

Cina.—*Chin.*, fainting fits. It proves successful to put a very tight ligature around the upper part of the arms and legs, in order to prevent the reflux of blood. But if one of the limbs is the affected part, it should not, of course, be applied to this one. The bandage should be left on, until after the bleeding has ceased for some time.

If an artery has been injured, it must be tied by a surgeon; till he comes, press a piece of cloth on the place where the blood issues, or press the artery a little above the injured place, with the fingers. Compare *external injury*.

7. Rheumatism, acute and chronic; stitch; pain in the hip and lameness.

Rheumatism attacks generally the muscles, but sometimes the joints; if the knee, it is always a feverish affection and liable, if neglected, to seize the heart. This disease, generally caused by taking cold, may or may not be attended by fever. When the muscles of the chest are affected, the disease is sometimes very easily confounded with pleurisy.

Acon., much fever; *Bell.*, swelling, inflammation; *Bryon.*, worse in motion; *Rhus*, worse in rest; *Merc.*, perspiration without relief, worse at night; *Puls.*, changing its place; *Arnica*, rheumatism of the back or chest; *Tart. emet.*, rheumatism of the joints; *Ars.*, striking to the heart; *Sulph.*, liability to rheumatism, chronic rheumatism. *Cham.*, *Nux*, *Chin.*

Stitch, a sudden attack of pain in the back, *Arn.*, chief remedy; *Rhus*, liability to it.

Pain in the hip and lameness. This disease is mentioned here to prevent mistake, as it may be an inflammation of the joint, particularly with children, and in such cases often without pain, (see lameness of children,) or it may be a neuralgia of the large nerve of the leg, or common rheumatism. If it is neuralgia, the pain usually extends to the knees and even to the heel, affecting particularly the back part of the whole leg. In this disease use *Puls.*, *Nux*, *Veratr.*, or *Bell.*

8. Gout.

Gout may be easily confounded with rheumatism, as it has often very similar symptoms. It is a disease of the whole system, although it attacks particularly the ends of the bones and the ligaments of the joints, where are formed gout-knots, which cause contractures and stiffness of the joints. The feet or hands are mostly attacked, especially with old people.

Particularly in acute attacks,—*Acon.*, fever; *Bell.*, redness; *Arn.*, *Merc.*, *Rhus*, *Bryon.*, *Puls.* Liability to the disease or when chronic, *Nux*, *Calc.*, *Sulph.*, *Acid. phosph.*

9. Scrofulous disease, swelling of the glands, goitre, rickets, rhachitis.

By scrofula is understood a chronic disease, which shows the following symptoms: frequent swelling of the glands, chronic diseases of the skin, chronic inflammation of the eyes, discharges from the ears, tendency to become fat and paunch-bellied, bloated nose, lips and face, liability to disordered digestion, as diarrhoæ, unnaturally craving appetite, peculiar desire to eat sand, chalk, coal, etc.; difficulty in learning to walk, weakness of the legs, etc. *Calc.*, *Sulph.*, *Silic.*, *Hep.*, *Merc.*

It is absolutely required to give light and easily digested, but nourishing food. Children should be taken out doors and allowed as much exercise as possible. Cold washing or cold bathing every day is very beneficial.

Swelling of the glands happens often with children. The swollen glands are sometimes painful, or otherwise. This affection is often attended by other symptoms of scrofula.

Merc., chief remedy when not very painful or during festering; *Bell.*, redness and great painfulness; *Acon.*, much inflammation; *Hep.*, festering; *Silic.*, slowly healing, fistulæ; *Sulph.* or *Calc.*, liability to the disease; *Carb.*, indurated glands in the groin.

Apply externally a warm (not medicinal) poultice; no salves, etc. Lancing is frequently required.

Goitre, struma is swelling and enlargement of the gland, lying before the throat, particularly with scrofulous persons, but in some countries epidemic, probably in consequence of the water. *Spong.*, chief remedy; *Hep.*, *Calc.*, *Silic.*

Rickets, rachitis is a scrofulous disease of the bones, which become softened, enlarged, crooked, and misformed. Consult a physician. *Calc.*, *Silic.*, *Merc.*

10. Scurvy.

Compare *scurvy in the mouth.* Beside the symptoms of the mouth, as mentioned under *scurvy in the mouth*, there are bluish red spots under the skin, caused by confined blood, which has escaped from the blood vessels; bleeding easily from the mouth, nose and other parts of the body; pain in the limbs; general weakness and debility; disordered digestion; sometimes fever. The disease prevails especially on the sea-coast and aboard vessels, and is caused by improper living, as eating much corned beef, salted meat and fish. Eat *fresh* meat and vegetables and drink lemonade once or twice a day.

Phosph. or *Acid. phosph.*, chief remedies. After having removed the disease, *China.*

11. Intermittent fever, chills and fever, ague.

This disease consists of three stages, viz: *cold stage*, *hot stage*, and *that of perspiration*, which is followed by an interval almost free from sickness, except great debility. The paroxysms occur every day or every third or fourth, and in most cases at the same hour. The ague prevails particularly during spring and fall in damp, flat countries, and is caused by sleeping too near the ground, being out doors after sunset, taking cold, or a faulty diet. It is in most cases easily cured by homœopathic medicine, but to select the right one, is sometimes very difficult.

The administration of large (allopathic) doses of *Quinine* is generally more injurious than beneficial, as it is the proper medicine in not more than one out of about twenty-five cases!

Quinine may often suppress the paroxysms, but without curing the disease.

During the paroxysm, give the medicine every hour; during the intervals, every two, three or four hours.

Ars., very violent paroxysms, long hot stage with great thirst, great debility, swollen limbs; *Puls.*, long cold stage, no thirst, chills or cold limbs in the intervals; *Nux*, susceptibility to cold, even in the hot stage; cold and hot stage not distinctly separated; disordered digestion; sallow complexion; *Veratr.*, very great debility, very pale face, collapse, diarrhœa, vomiting, slight hot stage; *Ignat.*, ague of slighter degree; cold and hot stage intermingled; after mental emotions; *Ipec.*, new cases, after faults in diet; symptoms of indigestion; *Chin.*, yellow face, distended abdomen, debility; *Cina*, craving appetite after, or at the end of the paroxysm, pale face; *Bryon.*, affection of the lungs.

These indications are not sufficient, as they are only a slight hint for the selection, compare therefore what is said upon these medicines in the Third Part.

12. Apparant death, lethargy, asphyxy.

It is often difficult to distinguish apparant, from real death, but the former is always to be supposed, especially with newborn children, as long as there are no certain signs of the latter. Immediately after death, the following indications begin to appear: (1.) dimness of the eyes; (2.) large red spots of escaped blood on those parts of the body, on which the person lay, when dying or immediately after; (3.) the anus not closed, but open. If boiling water be poured upon any portion of the skin, the place will become dry and transparent, but not inflamed as with living persons.

Do not become discouraged in performing the manipulations mentioned below, as it requires sometimes three, four, or even six hours or more before the patient is restored.

General rules.

1. Remove all clothing from the patient as gently as possible, if necessary, by cutting it off.
2. Place the patient in an easy, comfortable position, with the head high.
3. Rub the whole body, particularly the limbs, with warm cloths, keeping the trunk warm by hot ones, (except with frozen limbs or bodies).

4. Take care that the air of the room be pure and fresh. It often proves very successful, particularly with newborn children, to breathe air into the lungs, which may be done in the following manner: make some deep inspirations, put your mouth on that of the child, close its nose with your fingers, and slowly blow the air into its mouth; after that, press together the sides of the chest with your hands. This artificial respiration must be repeated continually, sometimes for one or two hours. If any delicacy is felt on the part of the operator, a piece of cloth may be placed over the mouth of the patient.

5. With the hanged, drowned or frozen, it proves useful to give at times a teaspoonful of water, in which is dissolved *Tart. emet.*, (one grain in a cup of water,) also to make injections of warm water and oil.

6. Avoid noise around the patient, resort to no bleeding, nor use too much strong smelling fluids.

Special rules.

1. *Apparent death of the newborn.* Clean the mouth and throat from the mucus. Sprinkle the body with æther or cold water alternated with

warm. Do not tie the navel string, unless these operations have proved unsuccessful, for the space of half an hour; it may then be dono, placing the infant in a warm bath, continuing there these manipulations. Give Opium every five or ten minutes.

2. *Apparent death caused by excessive mental emotions.* Uso tho proper medicino recommended under *mental emotions*, and compare what is said under *fainting fits.*

3. *Apparent death caused by external injury*, as a fall, blow, hanging, chocking ,etc. Dissolve *Arn.* in water and give a teaspoonful every half hour, or oftener.

4. *Apparent death caused by noxious vapors.* Take especial care for fresh air, by opening doors and windows, and sprinkle the face often with cold water or vinegar. *Coff.*, *Op.*, *Bell.*

5. *Apparent death caused by drowning.* Mouth and throat should be immediately cleansed and tho upper part of the body and head bent forward for a short time, in order that the water may flow out and a successful inclination to vomit be caused.

6. *Apparent death caused by freezing.* Tako great care in moving the body, because frozen

limbs break very easily. Either cover the whole body with snow, except the mouth and nose, or rub the whole surface with snow, but very gently, or put it in a bath of very cold water in a cold room, (heat, even moderate, would cause death,) till every part of the body becomes perfectly soft and pliable. Then put the patient in a bed and rub him with cotton or flannel; do not use heat, because the natural temperature must appear of itself in these cases. When slight signs of returning life manifest themselves, give at times a teaspoonful of the above mentioned solution of Tartar emetic and the lukewarm injections. When the patient begins to revive, give some teaspoonfuls of warm coffee. Heat must be avoided for a long time after recovery. For the violent pain after consciousness has returned, use *Carb.* or *Ars.;* if there is fever or headache, give *Acon.*

7. *Apparent death caused by hunger or thirst.* Make injections of warm milk or beef-broth, and give teaspoonfuls of the same internally in slow succession, as a much larger quantity, given at once, might cause death. When the patient feels some better, give a little wine, soft eggs, toast water or milk. After one or two days he may have some solid food. But

in no case must he be allowed to eat much at once for the first days; he may eat often, but a little at a time. If *thirst* is the cause, the treatment is very similar to this.

8. *Apparent death caused by lightning.* If possible, place the body in a hole, dug newly in the ground, or at least cover it all over with fresh earth, about two or three inches high. Give at times a teaspoonful of water, in which some globules of *Nux* have been dissolved. Make injections of warm water.

Compare *general illness with or without fever.*

13. Poisoning.

Although it is very difficult for non-professionals to treat a case of poisoning on account of the sciences of chemistry, physics, and botany being required, yet I mention here the treatment, because all these cases require the speediest aid.

There are two rules to be observed:

1. *Removal of the poison from the stomach, by vomiting, as soon as possible,* which is done best either by putting the finger in the throat, or drinking warm water, if necessary, mixed with butter or soap.

If the brain should be much affected, apply cold water to the head, and if the stomach or bowels, a warm poultice to the abdomen.

2. *If the poisonous article is* CERTAINLY KNOWN, *neutralization of it by giving the antidote*, which must be done as soon as most of the poison has been removed by vomiting. But as some poisons cause continual vomiting for a long time, the antidote should be administered, as soon as the greater part of the contents of the stomach has been thrown up, or at least, when the vomiting of mere phlegm commences.

If the poison is *unknown*, or *uncertain*, it is advisable to abstain from all powerful medicine including the below mentioned antidotes, to prevent still greater injury. Keep some of the discharges, first vomited, that the physician may ascertain the poison.

The best antidotes are the following:

POISONS.	ANTIDOTES.
Against *Alkalies*, (potassium, soda, ammonia, lime, lye.)	Vinegar, lemon juice.
" *Alum.*	Water and soap.
" *Antimony*, (tartar emetic.)	A decoction of nut-galls.
" *Arsenic.*	Hydrate peroxyde of iron, Magnesia.
" *Barytes.*	Glaubersalt, Epsom salt.
" *Copper*, (verdigris.)	Water containing the white of eggs, or sugar, Prussian blue.
" *Iodine.*	Starch.

POISONS.	ANTIDOTES.
Against *Lead.*	Epsom salt, (Sulphate of Magnesia.)
" *Lunar caustic*, (nitric silver.)	Table salt.
" *Oxalate of Potasse.*	Magnesia, Lime water.
" *Phosphorus.*	Mucilaginous drinks, Magnesia (*no* oil, butter, fat, etc.)
" *Quicksilver*, (Mercury.) Sublimate.	Water containing the white of eggs or sugar.
" *Sulphuric acid.*	Magnesia, pounded chalk, soda, much mucilaginous drinks.
" *Tin.*	Water containing the white of eggs, or sugar, milk.
" *Alcohol*, (brandy, rum, etc.)	Mucilaginous drinks and water containing Ammonia, (eight drops to one glass). Pouring of cold water over the head.
" *Camphor.*	Pouring of cold water over the patient; strong coffee.
" *Thorn Apple, Apple Peru.* (Strammonium.)	Strong coffee, vinegar, pouring of cold water over the patient.
" *Opium* or *Laudanum.*	Strong coffee, vinegar, pouring of cold water over the patient.
" *Henbane*, (Hyoscyamus.)	Pouring of cold water over the patient; strong coffee.
" *Mushrooms.*	Charcoal, diluted Ammonia, (eight drops to one glass of water.)
" *Deadly Nightshade*, (Belladonna.)	Strong coffee, pouring of cold water over the patient.
" *Prussic acid.*	Diluted Ammonia, (eight drops to one glass of water,) afterwards strong coffee.
" *Vomit-nut*, (Nux vomica,) or *Strychnine.*	Inhalations of Chloroform, Iodine dissolved in water; decoction of nut-galls; tannic acid; coal of meat.

POISONS.	ANTIDOTES.
Against *Poison of fishes.*	Charcoal, afterward strong coffee.
" *Poison of sausages, cheese, butter, meat.*	Vinegar, lemon juice, alkalies, pouring of cold water over the patient.
" *Spanish flies,* (Cantharides.)	Camphor, and mucilaginous drinks.

When the poison has been removed or neutralized in the above mentioned way, the patient is usually very sick, as some of the poison will have been absorbed, causing the disease. To cure this, use homœopathic remedies; therefore compare the following with what has been said under the proper head, as diseases of the stomach, bowels, etc. It is hardly necessary to mention, that the substance which caused the poisoning, can not be used afterwards in that case as a remedy.

Acon., fever, palpitation of the heart; *Coff.*, excitement, irritability, palpitation of the heart, sleeplessness; *Nux*, poisoning by deadly nightshade, lead, phosphorus, alcohol, rum; *Puls.*, want of appetite, bad taste, distress after eating, after poisoning by Sulphuric acid; *Ars.*, violent colic, burning pain, sensation of heat, diarrhœa, thirst, poisoning by Iodine; *Ipecac.*, nausea, vomiting, diarrhœa, want of appetite, poisoning by Opium or Arsenic; *Veratr.*, great distress and agony, nausea, cold perspiration, pale face; *Bell.*, liability to sudden fright, giddiness, headache, distention and painfulness of the stomach, poisoning by Iodine; *Coc.*, poisoning by Vomit-nut, Strychnine; *Sulph.*, poisoning by metals; *Hep.*, poisoning by metals, particularly Mercury, by sharp corroding substances; *Opium*, poisoning by lead, night-shade, camphor; *Carb.*, poisoning by alkalies; *Camph.*, poisoning by Prussic acid or Spanish flies; *Merc.*, poisoning by sharp, corroding substances.

Light, easily digested food.

Poisoning from the bite of poisonous animals, as snakes, mad dogs, etc. Wash the wound immediately after the bite, with water, then suck as strongly as possible the wound with your mouth for a quarter of an hour, pressing it at times with the fingers in order to force out the poison, (the sucked blood must be spit out,) finally wash carefully the wound with Ammonia or push in a pointed piece of lunar caustic, allowing it to remain for a few moments. If the bite of the animal is not very poisonous, washing the wound with Ammonia, vinegar or brandy is sufficient.

Use internally *Ars.*, *Rhus*, or *Bell.*

Poisoning from the touch of poisonous plants, as poison ivy, etc. Put rich earth on the affected part and renew it, whenever the pain increases. Washing with water and soap, or vinegar. Use internally *Rhus*, (except when caused by poison ivy,) *Bryon.* or *Bell.*, the former especially in cases of poisoning with poison ivy.

Poisoning by gas, see *apparent death*.

PART THIRD.

THE REMEDIES.

EXPLANATIONS OF THE SIGNS OF PARENTHESIS.

1. If ( ) are used, as for instance, under *Aconit*, "vomiting (bilious)," it means that *Acon. may* also be used in cases where the vomiting is not billious.

2. If [ ] are used, as for instance, under *Acon.*, "[rheumatism]," it means that *Acon.* may be used *only in cases, where all other symptoms, especially the characteristic ones, indicate its administration*, as *Acon.* is not a remedy for rheumatism, unless these conditions exist.

3. In cases where there is similarity between several remedies, they are frequently mentioned in parenthesis, to draw particular attention to a more careful selection. If therefore one remedy proves unsuccessful, give the other, which you

find mentioned, or at least consider it particularly in the next choice.

Aconitum napellus.

Chief remedy in the following cases:

1. *Rushing of blood* to any part or organ of the body, with or without hemorrhage, or *loss of blood* in general. The bleeding is sometimes, but the hemorrhage always attended by a full, hard, quick pulse.

2. *Inflammation* of any part or organ of the body with or without fever. By inflammation is understood painfulness, redness, swelling and increased heat of the affected part. It depends upon the importance of the affected part, on the intensity of the inflammation, and on the irritability of the patient, whether or not the inflammation is attended by fever, that is, full, hard, quick pulse, chills or heat with or without perspiration, thirst, or others of the below mentioned symptoms, (Bell., Bryon.) Likewise in cases of fever without any known inflammation; also when the blood is very much heated; or there is feverish uneasiness, agitation, (Bell., Coff.).

How long and how often *Acon.* should be given, depends entirely upon the intensity of the inflammation or of the fever. Give it in cases which can be treated by a non-professional, from every two to four hours, as long as there is much fever; when this begins to subside, give it alternately with the chief remedy of the disease, omiting it, when the fever has almost ceased. In a simple cold or hoarseness, etc., three or four doses are often sufficient; in other cases it may be given from two to three, four and five days.

3. *Pain* and *complaints* in general are *increased* by *motion*, (especially by *stooping*,) *noise*, and *pressure*, also in the evening and at night till after midnight.

4. In general *Acon.* suits particularly stout, strong, full-blooded persons.

GENERAL. Sleeplessness. (Coff.). [Rheumatism]. *Consequences of terror attended by vexation or of sudden joy.*

HEAD. Affection of the brain. Dullness,

NOTE. *Normal frequency of the pulse in one minute:* with newborn, 140–130; in the first year, 130–115; in the second, 115–100; in the third, 100–90; in the seventh, 90–85; in the fourteenth, 85–80; with grown persons, 75–70; with aged persons, 65–50. But this is not without exceptions. In high fever the frequency is increased to about double of the normal; but if increased only about one fifth, there is no fever at all. The pulse is the consequence of the action of the heart, there is therefore no difference between the beating of the pulse and of the heart in regard to frequency.

heaviness, fullnes, giddiness, pain, (Bell.). Sensation of pressure in the forehead.

FACE. Redness, heat. Bloatedness. Purple face, (Bell.). Crawling, stinging, jerking face-ache with a sensation, as if the part were swollen.

MOUTH. Toothache, almost insufferable, so that the patient is very much excited, (Coff.); throbbing, jerking toothache. [Teething].

STOMACH AND BOWELS. Want of appetite. Nausea, vomiting, (bilious). Costiveness. Painfulness.

LIVER. Jaundice of the newborn.

URINARY SYSTEM. Scanty, red, high colored urine; difficult, painful discharge of water with painful pressure upon the bladder. [Bloody discharges].

SEXUAL SYSTEM. [Terms too soon, too copious, too long; too painful labor].

THROAT AND CHEST. Tickling sensation in the throat. Hoarsness; sore throat, (Bell.). Light, hacking cough. Stinging pain in the chest, (Bryon.); dull pressure and heaviness. Dry cough or cough with a little tough mucous. Cough with bloody expectoration, (Arn.). Difficult, painful breathing, (Bryon., Bell.). Palpitation of the heart.

ARNICA MONTANA.

Chief remedy in the following cases:

After any kind of external injury, as a fall, blow, over-lifting, sprains, bruises, wounds, fractures, etc., after any operation, or too severe or too fatiguing exercise, or when in consequence of these external injuries there are *blood-shot spots*, *swelling*, *inflammation*, and *painfulness* of any part or organ of the body; moderate *fever*, (Acon.); *hemorrhage* or in general *loss of blood* from any part of the body, *fainting fits*, *palsy*, *apoplexy*, or apparent death.

In all these cases apply to the injured part cloth dipped in water, containing tincture of Arn., fifteen to twenty drops to half a pint of water.

GENERAL. Rheumatism with pain as if caused by sprains or bruises; the affected part is swollen, red, hard and shining. Rheumatism particularly of the small of the back and of the muscles of the chest.

SKIN. Boils.

HEAD. Affection of the brain; dullness, dizziness, pain, (Bell.). Pressure in the forehead. Pressing, stinging pain in the temples. Heat of the head and coldness of the body.

FACE. Swelling (hard and red,) of the cheek after removal of the toothache.

STOMACH AND BOWELS. Nausea, vomiting, (bilious).

URINARY SYSTEM. Difficult, painful discharge or retention of urine.

SEXUAL SYSTEM. [Terms too soon, too copious, too long]. Very violent afterpains after difficult and long protracted birth or operations; the tearing pain extends from the small of the back and groins to the inside of the thighs, attended by a constant desire to move the legs and a sensation as if the flesh was loosened from the bones.

CHEST. Pure blood easily raised. Difficult, painful breathing. Stinging pain and soreness when coughing or moving. Also useful in cases where the spitting of blood is not caused by external injury.

ARSENICUM ALBUM.

Particularly to be considered in the following cases:

1. When complaints are *periodic*, (Chin.)
2. When complaints appear or are increased *at night*.
3. When the pain is *burning*, piercing, *lancinating*.

4. When there is *hydropical swelling* of the limbs, face, or body in general; *dropsy* of the skin, or liability to it.

5. *Pale, haggard face.*

6. When there is great dryness of the mouth, *extreme thirst*, or inward, burning heat of the body.

7. When there is *great uneasiness, agitation, anguish, despair*, fear of death, sleeplessness.

8. Great *weakness* and *debility*, entire *prostration*, as long as the disease increases, or at least, does not disappear, (if the disease is disappearing, Chin. or Acid. phosph.); *rapid, great collapse*, (Veratr.)

9. *Very violent fever* in any disease with *feeble, intermittent pulse*, furious delirium, dry, blackish lips and tongue, fetid breath, involuntary discharges, bluish-red spots on the skin, etc., (Rhus,); (therefore frequently in later stages of diseases).

10. *Dark*, *thin*, (watery or bloody,) sharp, corrosive, *fetid* and *offensive smelling discharges* from any part or organ of the body.

11. When inflammation of any part or organ of the body threatens to change into gangrene,

or when there is *gangrene*, or *dark, black color* of the affected part.

12. *Cancer* of any part or organ of the body.

13. *Poisoning by the bite of venomous animals.*

GENERAL. Satiety of life and melancholy. Sleeplessness, (Coff.). *Ague*, increased by the abuse of Quinine; the paroxysms are distinguished by violence and long duration, especially the hot stage, which is attended by violent fever; profuse, long continued perspiration, usually appearing several hours after the hot stage; during the paroxysms there are frequently cramps, pains, delirium, palsy, all which disappear entirely during the intervals.

SKIN. Burns; scalds; nettle rash. [Boils; ulcers with hard, callous edges; small pox.]

HEAD. *Headache*, particularly on one side, better in the open air, worse in the house; throbbing headache. Painfulness of the scalp.

EYES. Inflammation, accompanied by great dread of light, burning, and secretion of acrid tears.

STOMACH AND BOWELS. Heart-burn. Eructations. Nausea, vomiting. Disordered stomach, especially if caused by fat, sour or too cold food.

Pain in the stomach. Vomiting of blood. *Griping colic.* Flatulency. *Diarrhœa*, particularly if soon after taking food and drinks, or after midnight; malignant cases of inflammation of the bowels, of dysentery, cholera, etc. Soreness of the anus, (Merc.).

SEXUAL SYSTEM. Too tardy appearance of the first terms. Terms too late, too scant, too short. Suppressions of the terms. Green-sickness.

NOSE, THROAT, AND CHEST. Cold with soreness of the nostrils and discharge of corrosive mucous. Dry, exhausting cough, increased by drinking or cold air. Moist cough, but without much expectoration. Very difficult breathing. *Spells of suffocation when lying down*, (Ipecac.). Sensation as if the throat and chest were pressed. Violent palpitation of the heart, less upon appearance of cough, (and expectoration). In many of these complaints the patient is forced to sit up and bend himself forward, or to lie in an erect position. Acute and chronic catarrh, asthma, inflammation of the heart.

LIMBS. *White swelling.*

BELLADONNA.

Particularly to be considered in the following cas

1. *Rushing of blood* to any part or organ of the body, but particularly to the *chest* and *head* —*flushed, purple face*—with or without *hemorrhage* or *loss of blood* in general; the bleeding is occasionally, but the hemorrhage always attended by a full, hard, quick pulse. The lost blood is generally of a light color.

2. *Inflammation* of any part or organ of the body with or without fever, under the following conditions:

(a) If the inflamed part looks *redder*, than in the cases for *Acon.*, almost *purple; dark redness*, sometimes radiating from one point, (Rhus,); very violent stinging, tearing pain, extending into the adjacent parts.

(b) Or if fever or inflammation is attended by *affection of the brain*, as dullness, *giddiness, pain, sleeplessness*, or *somnolency, delirium, madness, unconsciousness;* great uneasiness; *staring, rolling or fixed eyes; enlarged pupils.*

In the above cases used usually *after Acon.*, compare therefore what is said there.

3. Pain and *complaints* generally *are increased by motion*, (especially by stooping,) *pressure, noise*, and *bright light*, in the evening and at night, till after midnight.

4. *In various affections of the nervous sys-*

tem, as starting in the sleep and looking around as if terrified, frightful dreams, liability to sudden fright, jerking of the muscles, convulsions, lock-jaw, epilepsy.

5. *Affections of the throat* (Merc.,) *and gullet.*

6. In general *Bell.* suits particularly *stout, strong, full-blooded persons.*

GENERAL. Sleeplessness, (Coff.). Great desire to sleep, but inability. Sensitiveness to noise. *Redness, painfulness, and swelling of the glands*, (Acon., Merc.). Acute attacks of gout. *Acute rheumatism* with stinging, burning pain, swelling and redness of the affected part. Palsy. Fainting fits.

SKIN. *Erysipelas. Nettle rash. Scarlet fever.* Scarlet rash. French measles. Boils, etc.

HEAD. Besides the above mentioned symptoms of the brain are also the following: heaviness; fulness; pressing, stinging, throbbing pain. Sensation of pulsation and striking of the brain against the skull. Sensation as if the brain were jared. Pulsation in the temples. Heat of the head. Apoplexy. water in the head.

FACE. *Red, purple, flushed, hot, bloated face.* Face-ache, particularly near the eye. *Jerk-*

ing of the muscles and distortion of the features. Palsy of the muscles. Red and painful swelling of the nose. *Mumps*.

EARS. Pain, extending into the throat and head. Humming and buzzing in the ear. Hardness of hearing. Difficulty of hearing alternated with increased sensitiveness to noise. Discharge from the ear, particularly after diseases of the skin. Hardness of hearing, when the discharge has been suddenly suppressed.

EYES. Besides the above mentioned symptoms are the following: *Dread of light*. Sparkling or glimmering before the eyes. Dimness of the sight. The patient sees sparks and black spots. Running of (acrid) tears or disagreeable dryness. *Squinting*. Erysipelatous swelling of the eyelids. Paralysis of the eyelids.

MOUTH. Dryness. Stinging, tearing, drawing, throbbing toothache. [Teething]. Palsy of the tongue.

GULLET. *Difficult, painful swallowing*. Spasmodic, involuntary swallowing. Constant disposition to swallow.

STOMACH AND BOWELS. Heartburn. Retching. Nausea, vomiting but without much disorder of digestion. *Pain* in the stomach, extending back to the spine. The stomach sensitive to touch.

Griping colic. Griping, tearing pain in the bowels; during the pain a thick sausage-like swelling protrudes across the upper part of the abdomen, and, in bending over or by pressure upon it, the pain is somewhat relieved. Contracting pain under the navel. Distention and painfulness. (Thin, slimy stools). Cancer of the stomach.

URINARY SYSTEM. Difficult, painful passing of water. Too frequent discharges of water. Wetting of the bed. Palsy of the bladder. (Bloody discharges.)

SEXUAL SYSTEM. *Painful terms*, particularly when too late and scant or in consequence of the rushing of blood to the head—bleeding from the nose—and chest, (Bryon.); or when in consequence of the same cause the first terms appear too late.—*Strong bearing down in the lower part of the abdomen*, as if the parts would fall out. Terms too soon, too copious, too long. Hemorrhage. *Light colored blood.* Too painful labor, or natural one too seldom. *Puerperal fever* with suppressed secretion of milk and lochiæ.

THROAT AND CHEST. *Sore throat*, (Merc.). Much redness, swelling and pain. Sensation as if the throat was contracted. The throat swollen and sensitive to touch. Dryness. Palate and tonsils swollen and inflamed. Constant tickling in the windpipe. *Dry, spasmodic, convulsive cough*, shaking tho whole body and producing a splitting sensation in the head, sometimes with a very little expectoration. Barking cough, (Spong.). *Spitting of blood*, particularly when the flowing terms or piles have been suppressed. Sensation of tickling, throbbing in the chest. Difficult breathing and pressure, (Bryon.). Short and quick breathing, sometimes alternating with long breaths. *Palpitation of the heart*, causing quaking and throbbing in the head and neck.

BRYONIA ALBA.

Particularly to be considered in the following cases:

1. *Rushing of blood to the chest* and head with or without hemorrhage, or loss of blood in general.

2. *Inflammations*, particularly *of the internal parts, when the* STINGING *pain prevails* and there is *moderate fever*.

In the above mentioned cases given usually *after Acon.*, compare therefore *Acon.*, also *Bell.*

3. *Rheumatic complaints* particularly when the pain is increased by motion.

GENERAL. Uneasiness, (Cham.). *Nervousness and irritability*, (Coff.). *Rheumatism* of the muscles, the affected part being stiff or a little swollen, worse at night. *Consequences of anger and vexation*, (Nux).

HEAD. *Pain, particularly in the forehead.* Dullness, giddiness, increased by stooping. Slight delirium, (Bell.).

NOSE. Red, painful swelling, (Bell.). *Bleeding*, (Bell.).

MOUTH. Yellowish, coated tongue. Bitter taste. Blisters on the tongue. (Dryness in the mouth)

STOMACH AND BOWELS. Want of appetite. Bitter eructations. Nausea, vomiting, (Ipec.). Pressure and sensitiveness of the stomach. *Pain in the stomach*, (immediately after eating), worse in motion, better when lying down. *Stinging*, pressing pain in the abdomen. Flatulency. *Costiveness*, (Nux). *Diarrhœa*, particularly in summer after taking cold; (greenish or) brownish stools with (straining and) griping pain, (Merc.). Typhoid fever of minor degree.

LIVER. Jaundice.

URINARY SYSTEM. Muddy, dark, red urine.

SEXUAL SYSTEM. *Terms too soon, too copious, too long*, (Nux). Terms too late, too scant, too short, but bleeding from the nose or spitting of blood, (Bell.).—Too much secretion of milk, also suppression of its secretion, (Merc.).

CHEST. *Dry cough* or cough with a little tough mucous, (Bell., Nux), particularly in the morning and evening, sometimes with efforts to vomit, or with shooting pains in the head and chest. *Stinging* pain. Sensation of soreness.

LIMBS. (Palsy of the legs).

CALCAREA CARBONICA.

Particularly to be considered in the following cases:

1. *Scrofulous disease* (Hep., Sulph., Merc., Silic.), as swelling or induration of the glands, etc.

2. *Chronic catarrh** of any mucous membrane, as cold, cough, diarrhœa, whites, or *liability to it*, (Hep., Sulph., Merc.).

---

* The *mucous membrane* is the thin, transparent, reddish skin, which covers the eyeball and lines the eyelids, nose, lips, tongue, mouth, throat, windpipe and its ramifications, the cells of the lungs, gullet, stomach and intestines to the anus, the urethra, bladder, passage to the kidneys, the vagina and womb. It secrets a slimy, slippery mucous. Any part of this membrane can be attacked by catarrhal inflammation, acute as well as chronic. In the first stage of the *acute catarrhal inflammation*, the natural secretion of the mucous is suppressed, the membrane inflamed and swollen. The inside of the

3. *Old sores and festers* of any part or organ of the body.

4. *Calc.* suits particularly *feeble, pale,* or *fat, paunch-bellied, bloated, scrofulous persons, especially children;* also, in *liability to become fat,* or in cases of *sudden emaciation,* often without any known cause and in spite of a good appetite.

General. Great weakness. Nervous exhaustion. Chronic epilepsy, particularly at night. Gout. Occasional flashes of heat.

Head. Pressing, throbbing, drawing *headache* in one side, particularly in the morning. Sensation of heaviness of the head with pressure

---

nose, for instance, feels disagreeably dry and the free passage is impeded. In the second and third stage the inflammation is lessened, but the secretion of mucous considerably increased. If the mucous membrane lines organs, where nothing but air has admittance, the discharge consists of mere phlegm; but if it lines organs, where this is not the case, the mucus will be mixed with what these organs contain. If the inflammation, for instance, attacks the mucous membrane of the intestines, the mucous will be mixed with the food and will appear in the shape of diarrhœa, which will be the more profuse, the more freely the phlegm is discharged.—The *chronic catarrh* differs from the acute as follows:

1. The inflammation is generally slight and the pain frequently entirely absent.
2. The quantity of mucous is less than in acute catarrhal inflammations.
3. It may last any length of time.

Acute catarrh frequently changes into chronic.

Catarrh is a shorter expression for catarrhal inflammation, both meaning the same.

upon the eyes. Occasional rushing of blood to the head. Sensation of icy coldness of the head. Painfulness of the scalp. With infants large heads with open fortanels. Losing of the hair.

FACE. Pale, wan face, but sometimes flushed.

EYES. Indurated sty. Secretion of sticky mucous, (Hep.). Dimness of the sight with aged persons.

NOSE. Swelling of the nose and upper lip, (Hep.). Chronic stoppage of the nose caused by swelling of the mucous membrane, (Merc.). *Polypus.* Eruptions on the nose.

MOUTH. Liability to toothache with pregnant females. *Slow and difficult teething.*

STOMACH AND BOWELS. (Sour) eructations. Heartburn. Nausea, vomiting. Craving appetite. Waterbrash. Loathing of meat and warm food. Craving for sour and piquant food. Sour stomach. Swelling and sensitiveness of the stomach, (Hep.). Liability to worms, (Sulph.). *Chronic diarrhœa* without pain, (Acid. phosph., Chin.). Thick, bloated, hard abdomen.

SEXUAL SYSTEM. Emissions. *Terms too soon, too long, too copious. Whites. Terms, suppressed or scant. Green-sickness.*

CHEST. *Chronic cough.* Dry cough with violent tickling as if caused by dust, particularly at night. Cough with thick, yellowish (offensive smelling,) expectoration, (causing a rattling sound). Consumption. Palpitation of the heart.

Spine. Weakness, especially when sitting.

Limbs. *Difficulty in learning to walk.* Great weakness of the legs. Crooked bones.

Cantharides.

Skin. *Burning* pain, (Ars.). Burns and scalds.

Tongue. Inflammation.

Bowels. Inflammation with burning, cutting pain, (Bell.).

Urinary system. *Very difficult, painful passing of water. The water passing only by single drops. Sharp pain in the bladder.* Bloody, slimy discharges. Palsy of the bladder.

Sexual system. *Extreme sexual excitement with great sexual desire.* Frequent and long continuing erections. Frequent emissions. Lascivious dreams.

Carbo vegetabilis.

Skin. Ulcers with burning pain and fetid smell, bleeding easily.

EAR. Dryness of the auditory passage.

NOSE. Easily bleeding, (Phosph.). Scabs or red spots on the tip of the nose. Copper-nose.

MOUTH. Scurvy in the mouth. Easily bleeding. Putrid smelling.

STOMACH AND BOWELS. Heartburn. Nausea. Vomiting. Loathing of all food. Disordered stomach caused by spirituous drinks. Vomiting of blood, (Ipec.). Burning, contracting pain, particularly after flatulent food. *Chronic distention of the abdomen by wind*, (without pain,) (Chin., Sulph.). (Painless diarrhœa). *Pulseless, asphyctic cholera* with coldness of the whole body, cold perspiration, violent thirst.

URINARY SYSTEM. Wetting of the bed.

THROAT AND CHEST. Chronic *hoarseness* and *aphony*, particularly in the morning and evening. *Husky voice*. Dry, hoarse cough with itching, tickling, and burning in the throat and chest. Spasmodic cough increased by speaking and bad weather. Cough with whitish, greenish expectoration.

LIMBS. Indurated glands in the groin.

CHAMOMILLA VULGARIS.

GENERAL. *Cham. suits particularly females*

and children. Most complaints are worse at night. Moderate fever with heat and thirst, or chills. Weakness. *Uneasiness, tossing about.* Ill-humor. Excitement, *irritability.* Sleeplessness, or broken, unquiet sleep. Inclination to weep. Slight convulsions, (Bell.). Consequences of vexation and anger. Pain in the small of the back, with a sensation as if broken, (Nux.). Tearing, drawing rheumatism with a sensation of numbness in the affected part, relieved for a little while by sitting up, or motion. Crying of infants.

SKIN. Soreness, excoriation. Scabs.

HEAD. Tearing, jerking headache, extending into the cheek and teeth, particularly after taking cold. Dullness. Perspiration. Sometimes rushing of blood with heat.

FACE. *One pale and one red cheek.* Red face. (Pale face). Blue circles around the eyes, (Cina.).

EARS. Insufferable stinging pain. Dryness and a sensation as if obstructed.

EYES. Burning pain. Slight redness.

NOSE. Cold with sore nostrils, accompanied by cracked, inflamed, sore lips.

MOUTH. *Toothache* in the whole side, extending into the ear and face, without affecting

caused through a draught.

one particular tooth, increased by drinking something warm. Bitter taste. Coated tongue. [Teething].

STOMACH AND BOWELS. No appetite. Loathing of food Bitter eructations. Vomiting of greenish, bitter mucous. Pain in the stomach, sometimes alleviated by drawing one's self up. *Griping colic.* Tearing, drawing pain in the bowels. Wind, pent up in different parts of the abdomen, with a sensation as if about to escape. Distention of the abdomen. Rattling and rumbling with disposition to evacuate. *Diarrhœa*, slimy, watery, *like curdled milk, but of a yellowish* (greenish,) *color*.

LIVER. Jaundice of the newborn.

URINARY SYSTEM. Painful, difficult passing of water.

SEXUAL SYSTEM. *Terms too soon, too copious, too long. Painful terms* with sensitiveness of the whole abdomen. Painful pressure like labors, from the small of the back downward or forward. *Hemorrhage* with periodical pain. *Dark, thick, coagulated blood.—Too painful labor.*

THROAT AND CHEST. Sore throat, (Bell.). Slight redness and swelling. Sensation as if something were in the throat, with a constant, but ineffectual desire to remove it. Tickling, burning pain. Dryness and uncomfortable feeling in the throat. Hoarseness, (Merc.). Irritation to cough. Dry cough or cough with a little tough mucous. Short, noisy respiration. Difficult breathing. Palpitation of the heart.

LIMBS. Trembling and spasmodic jerks, (Bell.).

CHINA OFFICINALIS.

Particularly to be considered in the following cases:

1. *Weakness and debility*, caused by loss of blood, nursing, severe or weakening diseases, sexual intercourse, self-pollution, etc., *and their consequences*, as bleeding, hemorrhage, feeble digestion, fainting fits, convulsions, etc., (Acid. phosph.).
2. *Periodical complaints*, (Ars.).
3. *Many of the complaints appear, or are increased at night.*

GENERAL. Slight fever *with weak pulse*, heat or chills. Hemorrhage with fainting fits, coldness and paleness of the body. When during festering of any part, chills, perspiration, great irritability and extreme exhaustion make their appearance, (Carb.). Frequent perspiration. Drowsiness. Sleeplessness. Disturbed, broken sleep. Uneasiness. *Ague*, caused by direct influence of miasma; relaxation and weakness during and after the paroxysms; thirst usually between the cold and hot stage, or after the latter, during the perspiration; hot and cold stage often alternating, or heat a long while after the latter.

HEAD. Dullness, giddiness. Pain. Occasional rushing of blood, causing swollen veins on the forehead. Losing of the hair.

FACE. Prickling, jerking, stinging, cutting, burning neuralgic pain, increased by touch, lessened by eating. Pale, wan, faded, yellowish face. Jerking of the muscles of the face.

EYES. Slight inflammation. Weakness. Momentary blindness. Dimness of the sight.

NOSE. Bleeding.

MOUTH. *Toothache*, increased by eating, touch of the finger and cold air, alleviated by pressing the teeth together.

STOMACH AND BOWELS. Want of appetite. Heartburn. Ravenous appetite. Craving for sour or piquant food. *Constant feeling of having eaten to satiety. Food causing pressure in the stomach.* Regorgitation. Pain in the stomach. Nausea; vomiting of undigested food. Desire to lie down after every meal. *Sensation of fulness.* Eructation and emission of wind affording relief. Sensation of coldness in the abdomen. *The bowels very much distended by wind*, particularly after eating, especially of flatulent food. Rumbling. Slight griping colic. (Painless, chronic) *diarrhœa.* The discharges mixed with undigested food. Costiveness, the discharge being preceded by an ineffectual inclination to evacuation, and attended by straining and pain in the anus. After frequent use of emetics or aperients.

LIVER. Jaundice, particularly after having taken too much Mercury.

URINARY SYSTEM. Dark, muddy, scant urine.

SEXUAL SYSTEM. Emissions. The terms too late, too scant, too short. Too tardy appearance of the first terms. Greensickness. Whites, particularly before and after the terms. *Bleeding, hemorrhage.*

CHEST. Spitting of blood with (violent) cough. Palpitation of the heart.

LIMBS. Trembling. Jerking of the hands.

CINA.

GENERAL. *Cina suits particularly* (paunch-bellied) *children, suffering from worms, especially from pin-worms.* Uneasy sleep. *Ague* with thirst during the cold stage. Convulsions, (Bell.).

FACE. Pale, faded face. *Blue circles around the eyes.*

EYES. Dilated pupils.

NOSE. Disposition to pick the nose. Violent bleeding. Danger of bleeding to death.

STOMACH AND BOWELS. Want of appetite. Craving appetite. Ravenous appetite, frequently even after vomiting. Tendency to vomit. Vomiting.

URINARY SYSTEM. Wetting of the bed.

CHEST. *Dry, spasmodic, convulsive cough.* The patient, during the coughing, becomes quite stiff, the paroxysm being succeeded by a gurgling sound, which seems to descend from the throat into the abdomen.

COCCULUS INDICUS.

GENERAL. *Faintness.* Groaning. Sighing. Uneasiness. Convulsions. The patient despondent, sullen and taciturn. *Sea-sickness.*

HEAD. Giddiness. Ringing. Sensation as if one were drunk. Headache, particularly after eating, drinking, or mental exertion.

Ear. Buzzing. Hardness of hearing.

Stomach and bowels. *Nausea. Vomiting.* Griping, pressing, jamming pain in the stomach and bowels.

Sexual system. *Painful, scant terms* with pressing pain, like colic, and pressure on the chest.

Limbs. Palsy of the arms.

Coffea arabica.

Particularly to be considered with *sensitive, irritable, nervous persons,* especially with females and children, or when there is *excitement, sensitiveness, irritability,* caused by pain, disease, mental emotions, etc., also by their consequences, as palpitation of the heart, diarrhœa, fainting fits, etc.

General. Excessive liveliness. *Sleeplessness.* Extreme sensitiveness to noise. Great agitation. Uneasiness. Liability to sudden fright. Inclination to weep. Excessive pain causing grinding of the teeth, crying, groaning, trembling, coldness, numbness, and stiffness of the body.

Head. Giddiness. Headache as if the brain were rent and crushed. One sided headache.

MOUTH. Toothache. [Teething].

STOMACH AND BOWELS. Heartburn. [Nausea; vomiting; diarrhœa].

SEXUAL SYSTEM. *Painful terms* with a sensation in the abdomen, as if it would burst. Terms too long, too soon, too *copious*. Too painful labor.

CHEST. Short, difficult breathing. Asthma. Palpitation of the heart.

COLOCYNTHIS.

GENERAL. (Uneasiness; excitement; tossing about). Strong smelling perspiration.

HEAD. Dullness. Very violent tearing, one-sided, periodical headache, particularly in the afternoon. Pressure in the forehead, increased by stooping and lying down.

FACE. Tearing, burning, stinging pain, extending into the ear and head, or gnawing, burning pain in the bones of the cheek (Silic.) with swelling and redness, worse in rest, than in motion.

STOMACH AND BOWELS. Nausea, vomiting. *Griping colic*, so *violent* as to force the patient to bend double; the pain somewhat relieved by pressing the abdomen with the hands. *Insufferable jamming, pressing, cutting pain*, appearing usually in single spells, and being most violent about the navel; after an attack of pain, a sensation as if the bowels were torn and broken. Fullness and distention of the abdomen. Sensation of emptiness. Violent, exhausting, slimy, bloody diarrhœa.

URINARY SYSTEM. Muddy, *strong smelling* urine.

LIMBS. (Cramps of the calves of the legs).

DIGITALIS PURPUREA.

HEART. Strong, almost audible palpitation with great uneasiness and cramp-like pain in the breast-bone, and occasionally slow pulsation of the heart.

HEPAR SULPHURIS.

Particularly to be considered in the following cases:

1. *Consequences of having taken too much Mercury*, as salivation, ulceration, etc.

2. *Scrofulous disease*, (Calc., Sulph., Silic., Merc.).

3. *Chronic catarrh of any mucous membrane*, as cold, cough, inflammation of the eyes, diarrhœa, whites, *or liability to it*, (Calc., Sulph.,

Merc.). Explanation of catarrh, see under *Calcarea.*

4. *Festering* of any part or organ of the body, (Merc., Sulph., Calc., Silic.).

General. Sensitiveness to cold air. Struma.

Skin. Scabs, particularly on the face or scalp. Runrounds. Felon. Ulcers. Eczema.

Ears. Running from the ear. Buzzing and hardness of hearing, particularly after suppressed running from the ear.

Eyes. Inflammation, especially if chronic. Soreness and swelling of the edges of the eyelids with secretion of thick mucous, like matter. Adhering of the eyelids at night. Ulcers and spots on the cornea. Eyelids turned inside out.

Nose. Chronic cold. Stoppage, caused by swelling of the mucus membrane. Swelling of the nose and upper lip. Eruptions. Scabs.

Mouth. Much secretion of saliva.

Stomach and bowels. Foul, fetid eructation. Nausea, particularly in the morning. Vomiting of mucous, bile or sour substances. Craving for sour or stimulating food. Frequent disordered digestion in spite of the most regular diet. Chronic (painless) diarrhœa, or liability to it.

Urinary system. Wetting of the bed.

THROAT AND CHEST. (Chronic) *hoarseness.* Sore throat, (Merc.). Liability to sore throat. Tickling in the throat. Much loose, moist cough with rattling of mucous and inclination to vomit, (Tart. emet.). Much loose, *tough* mucous in the throat and windpipe. Whistling breathing. Difficult breathing.

IGNATIA AMARA.

Particularly to be considered in the following cases:

1. With *nervous, sensitive, irritable, timid* (unmarried) *persons, especially females,* also with children.
2. *In various affections of the nervous system,* as great excitement, sudden startling, trembling, spasmodic jerks, piercing cries when asleep, nightmare, convulsions, epilepsy, Saint Vitus's dance, (Bell.).
3. *Consequences of* terror, *grief, sorrow, mortification, home-sickness.*

GENERAL. Sleeplessness, (Coff.). Very changeable disposition of the mind, from joy to sorrow. Depression of the mind. *Ague,* during the paroxysms frequent sudden alternation of coldness and heat, or they occur together, or one part is affected by coldness and the other by heat; thirst exists only in the cold stage; the coldness being easily relieved by external warmth.

SKIN. *Itching* as if caused by fleas, particularly at night and without any visible disease of the skin.

HEAD. Throbbing headache. Sensation as if the head were pressed apart. Pressing pain above the root of the nose, alleviated by bending the head forward.

FACE. Paleness.

EYES. Dread of light. Momentary blindness. Inflammation. Secretion of mucous.

STOMACH AND BOWELS. Eructations. *Hiccough.* Nausea, vomiting. An obstacle or pain is felt during the swallowing of food, as if it were unable to pass the gullet, or as if squeezed through a painful place, (Phosph.). Pain in the stomach. *Itching in the anus*, caused by worms.

URINARY SYSTEM. Much watery urine.

SEXUAL SYSTEM. *Painful terms.*

CHEST. Dry, convulsive cough. Palpitation of the heart.

Ipecacuanha.

Particularly to be considered in the following cases:

1. *Catarrh of the stomach* and bowels. (Explanation of catarrh, see under *Calcarea*).

2. *Spasmodic affections of the chest* with spells of suffocation (Ars.), accompanied with paleness, coldness or cold perspiration, and stiffness of the body (Cina.) with or without cough.

3. *Violent bleeding or hemorrhage* from any part or organ of the body, or *danger of bleeding to death*.

General. Weakness. Drowsiness. Disposition to lie down. *Ague*, caused by faults in diet, attended by disorder of the stomach, bowels and chest, which exists especially before and during the hot stage; the cold feeling is more internal than external, lasts long and is often increased by application of heat; thirst during the hot stage, but very slight or none during the cold.

Head. Stinging, tearing pain, particularly in the forehead, increased by motion and touch. Sensation as if the brain and the bones of the head were bruised. Dullness.

FACE. Paleness. Blue circles around the eyes, (Cina.).

MOUTH. Tongue, coated in most cases. Bad taste. Saliva collecting in the mouth.

STOMACH AND BOWELS. Loathing of all food and smoking. *Nausea. Retching. Vomiting.* Fullness and pressure in the stomach after the eating of food. *Colic pain. Pain around the navel. Diarrhœa.* Straining. Tenesmus, (Merc.).

URINARY SYSTEM. Frequent desire to make water and passing of a little pale water.

THROAT AND CHEST. Sensation in the throat as if contracted. *Loose cough.* Loose *cough causing retching* and *vomiting*, (Tart. emet.). *Violent choking, suffocating cough*, causing flushes of blood to the head, throbbing in the head, and pressure upon the bladder, (Bell., Cina.). *Involuntary emissions of urine during coughing.* Dry, *convulsive cough*, (Bell.). *Spasmodic pressure in the chest*, as if the inhaled air could not be breathed out. Oppression in the chest, as if caused by inhalation of dust. Inspiration without difficulty, but not the expiration. Quick, sighing breathing. *Asthma.* especially at night, (Ars.). Rattling in the chest, (Tart. emet.).

Mercurius solubilis Hahnemanni.

Particularly to be considered in the following cases:

1. *Acute or chronic catarrh of any mucous membrane, if the former is not attended by much fever or inflammation, and the latter of not too long standing.* Explanation of catarrh see under *Calcarea.*

2. *Festering*, or *matter-like discharges* from any part or organ of the body, if the pain is not very violent, (Hep., Calc., Sulph.).

3. *Scrofulous disease*, especially swelling or ulceration of the glands.

4. *Syphilis.*

5. *Many complaints are worse in* (feather) *bed at night.*

6. *Liability to profuse perspiration, particularly in the last part of the night, or early in the morning; the patient receives no relief from it, but experiences great weakness.*

Persons who have frequently taken large doses of Mercury under allopathic treatment, may use *Hepar* instead of Mercury, if the latter does not suit them.

General. Rheumatism with swelling of the

affected part. Gout. Tumefaction or enlargement of the bones. Ulceration of the bones.

SKIN. Blisters, scabs particularly on the face and head. *Ulcers*, deep, dark, ill-looking, with much festering. Excoriations. *Fellon. Boils. Pustules. Small pox.*

HEAD. Dullness. Headache. Perspiration.

FACE. Neuralgia, extending into the teeth, attended by swelling. Swelling of the upper lip.

EARS. *Bloody* or *thin, offensive smelling*, or *mattery discharge* with little or no pain. *Soreness* of the auditory passage. Humming, buzzing. Noise like that of the pulse. Loud resonance of the tones. Sensation of obstruction, disappearing by swallowing or blowing the nose. Hardness of hearing. Tearing, stinging earache, extending into the cheek and teeth.

EYES. Pain. *Soreness.* Swelling. Inflammation. *Much secretion of mucous or matter.* Ulcers, spots on the cornea. *Soreness and swelling of the edges of the eyelids with secretion of thick mucous*, like matter. *Adhering of the eyelids at night.* The eyelids turned inside out. Blisters and scabs around the eyes.

NOSE. *Cold with much sneezing* and *running of water. Secretion of much thick mucous.*

Soreness. Redness. Painfulness. Swelling. Ulceration of the bones with secretion of offensive mucous or matter, (ozæna). Bleeding.

MOUTH. *Ulcers. Ulceration.* The gum spongy, swollen, ill-colored, separated from the teeth, and easily bleeding. *Fetid breath.* Scurvy. *Salivation*, or *collecting of saliva.* Thrush. *Toothache, caused by hollow teeth.* Toothache with pain extending into the ear and eye. Sensation as if the teeth were too long. Inflammation of the tongue. Coated tongue. Bad taste.

STOMACH AND BOWELS. Loathing of food, especially sweet. Nausea. Craving appetite. Hardness of the abdomen. Pain in the bowels. *Slimy, greenish*, or *bloody diarrhœa. Very painful and violent straining and tenesmus* before and after the discharge, as if the bowels were being torn out. *Soreness of the anus.*

LIVER. Jaundice.

URINARY SYSTEM. Painful, difficult passing of water. Passing of water only by single drops, (Canth.). Bloody, slimy discharges.

SEXUAL SYSTEM. Swelling of the testicles. *Whites* with secretion of very acrid mucus, causing soreness and sensitiveness of the private parts. Delay of the appearance of the milk.

THROAT AND CHEST. The tonsils uneven, slight red or yellowish. Pain in the throat, extending into the ear. *Sore throat. Hoarseness.* Redness, swelling and pain of the back part of the mouth and throat. *Difficult swallowing.* Burning, tickling sensation in the throat. Husky voice. Moist cough. Expectoration of thick, mattery mucous.

NUX VOMICA.

Particularly to be considered in the following cases:

1. *Affections of the spine, i. e.* of the spinal marrow.

2. *Affections of the stomach and bowels,* (disordered digestion with inclination to costiveness,) *and in consequence of this, affection of the brain,* as dullness, headache, rushing of blood to the head, and *affection of the spirits and mind,* as ill-humor, hypochondriasis, etc.

3. When there is *ill-humor, passionate, impatient disposition of the mind.*

4. When *complaints have been caused by sedentary habits, too great mental application, drinking coffee, wine, spirituous drinks, use of tobacco, debauch, etc.*

5. When *complaints are worse in the morning or forenoon, better in the afternon and evening.*

6. When *complaints are aggravated by motion or walking in the open air.*

7. *In general Nux suits especially dark-haired and -eyed persons, of a sanguinic or choleric temper, and particularly males of this character.*

If there is no great necessity of taking *Nux immediately*, take it in the evening before going to bed, as it will operate the better, if taken at this time.

GENERAL. Disinclination for work or business. Sleeplessness, (Coff.). *Nightmare.—Gout. Varicose veins.* Consequences of vexation or anger, (Byron.). In cases of *ague* similar to those of *Ipecac*, but of longer standing and greater violence; there is emaciation, great debility, yellowish, gray complexion, very disordered digestion, variation of the stages, viz., the cold stage is frequently indistinctly separated from the hot, but often combined,—or the heat occurs before the coldness,—or external heat and internal coldness, or the reversal; the patient wishes to be covered even during the hot stage and that of perspiration, as he very easily feels chilly.

HEAD. Dullness. Giddiness. Pain. Pressing heaviness. Sensation as if the brain were bruised. Sensation of reverberating or trembling of the brain at every step.

FACE. Tearing, drawing face-ache, extending into the ear with swelling. Redness of the face.

EARS. Tearing, stinging ear-ache. Painful shocks. Tingling sensation. Creaking sound in moving the jaws. Loud sound of one's own words.

EYES. Slight inflammation, particularly of the inward corner. Pressing or burning pain. (Weakness.) Much flowing of tears. (Dread of light).

NOSE. Catarrh. Stoppage, particularly with infants. Bleeding.

MOUTH. Toothache increased by cold, lessened by heat. Sensation as if the tooth were being extracted, or as if the teeth were too long or loose. Pain in the whole side. Coated tongue. *Sour, bitter taste.* Collecting of saliva.

STOMACH AND BOWELS. *Want of appetite. Heartburn.* Craving appetite. *Eructations.* Nausea, vomiting. *Pressing, griping, contracting pain* in the stomach, usually after eating.

Fullness and swelling of the stomach after eating. *The bowels much bloated*, causing difficult breathing. Oppression as if caused by a bandage around the body. Desire to open the clothing, which is burdensome. Rumbling, rolling. Griping colic. Pressure on the bladder and rectum, as if wind would force itself from these places, *Costiveness*. Hard fæces. Frequent but unsuccessful desire to evacuate. Sensation as if the anus were closed. *Piles*, (Sulph.).

Urinary system. Difficult, painful passing of water, especially after forced suppression. Palsy of the bladder.

Sexual system. Swelling and painfulness of the back part of the testicles and of the seminal cord, (Puls.). Frequent erections and emissions. Great sexual desire. *Terms too soon, too copious, too long*, (Calc., Bryon.), too painful, (Bell.). Writhing pain. Hemorrhage.

Throat and chest. Slight inflammation of the throat, (Bell., Merc.). Sore throat. Slight hoarseness. *Tickling, or sensation as if the throat were scratched inside.* Sensation of swelling as if the throat were narrowed or a lump were there. Rough and scraping sensation in the throat. *Dry, hacking cough, caused by a tickling sensation in the throat,* appearing upon the slightest occasion, as speaking, drinking, etc. The spells of coughing are sometimes very violent, as if the chest and head would burst, (Bell.), with efforts to vomit, (Ipecac.). Sometimes a very little mucous is discharged with difficulty. Asthma, with cramp-like pressure on the chest, causing great uneasiness, (Ars.). Palpitation of the heart.

Opium.

General. Sleeplessness, particularly with aged persons, (Coff.). Lascivious dreams. Fainting fits. Trembling, jerking of the muscles. Nightmare. Convulsions. Epilepsy, particularly at night. Palsy. Consequences of terror or fear. Chronic lead-poisoning, (Nux.)

Head. Dullness, giddiness, as if after intoxication, particularly when stooping. Rushing of blood to the head. Pain. Apoplexy. Somnolency. Unconsciousness, stupor with slow and snoring respiration, and strong, but slow, intermittent pulse.

Face. Paleness. *Redness.* Purple face. Jerking of the muscles.

Eyes. Red, glassy eyes. Dimness of sight. Dilated pupils.

Mouth. Dryness, thirst.

Gullet. Difficult swallowing, (Bell.).

Stomach and bowels. Want of appetite. Loathing of food. Nausea. *Costiveness*, particularly after weakness or relaxation of the intestines by aperients. Inclination, but no pressure, to an evacuation, accompanied with a sensation as if the anus were closed. Sensation of throbbing and heaviness. Carcerated or strangulated hernia, attended by vomiting of a substance smelling like fæces.

Sexual system. Erections and emissions. Ceasing of the labors.

Chest. Dry, convulsive cough. Palpitation of the heart.

Phosphorus.

General. Easy bleeding from any part of the body. In the later stages of severe diseases, when there is delirium, dry lips and tongue, involuntary discharges, cold, clammy perspiration, sudden loss of strength, etc.

Skin. Red spots or stripes.

Head. Giddiness, particularly in the morning and evening. Headache. Rushing of blood.

Ears. Buzzing and hardness of hearing, particularly after typhoid fever. Sensation of roaring. Loud resonance of the words and tones. Aversion to noise.

NOSE. Easily bleeding.

MOUTH. Swollen, ill-looking, easily bleeding gums. Scurvy.

STOMACH AND BOWELS. Sour eructations. Heartburn. Nausea. Rising of food. Pain in the gullet, (seemingly deep in the chest), when swallowing. Disordered digestion, particularly after the eating of too cold food. Distress after every meal. Pain in the stomach. Pressing, burning pain and heat in the stomach, extending up to the mouth. Distention of the abdomen. Watery, (bloody,) diarrhœa. Piles.

SEXUAL SYSTEM. Frequent erections and emissions, sometimes painful. Sexual excitement and great sexual desire. Too tardy appearance of the first terms. *The terms appearing too late, but more profuse and of longer duration*, followed by great weakness, emaciation, etc. Pain before the terms. Greensickness.

THROAT AND CHEST. *Chronic hoarseness or aphony*, (Carb.). Stinging pain and sensitiveness in the throat. Rushing of blood to the chest. Soreness, pressure and fullness. Stinging pain, particularly when moving or coughing.

Short breathing. *Danger of suffocation.* Irritation to cough, increased by speaking, laughing, etc. Dry cough. Cough with sticky, greenish or yellowish mucous. *Bloody expectoration.* Sensation as if hot blood came up to the throat. Palpitation of the heart.

ACIDUM PHOSPHORICUM.

GENERAL. Particularly to be considered in *great weakness*, *debility*, *exhaustion* and *their consequences*, as giddiness, palpitation of the heart, etc.

HEAD. Giddiness. Dullness. Pain. Humming in the ears. Weakness of the eyes.

MOUTH, STOMACH AND BOWELS. Aphthæ. Scurvey. Want of appetite. Pressure in the stomach. Rumbling. *Chronic*, *painless*, *watery diarrhœa.* The discharges are sometimes repressed with difficulty, sometimes involuntary.

SEXUAL SYSTEM. Emmissions in consequence of weakness, caused by too frequent sexual intercourse or self-pollution. Too tardy appearance of the first terms. Terms too short, too scant, too late. Greensickness.

CHEST. Bad tasting and smelling expectoration in the morning, but usually dry cough during the day-time. Palpitation of the heart.

Pulsatilla pratensis.

Particularly to be considered in the following cases:

1. *Catarrh of any mucous membrane with much secretion of a thin, not corrosive, mucous,* as cold, cough, diarrhœa, whites, etc. Explanation of catarrh, see under *Calcarea.*

2. *When complaints appear or are worse in the afternoon or evening, and cease or are better in the morning or forenoon.*

3. *When complaints are unattended by thirst; when the seat of the pain changes easily and often; when there is inclination to weep.*

4. *Puls. suits especially weak, pale, bloodless,* (frequently including those who are even fat or corpulent), *chilly, mild, good-natured, quiet, phlegmatic, light-haired people, particularly females and especially those whose terms are scant or with whom they have entirely ceased.* It suits also many complaints of green-sickness, pregnancy and hysterics.

General. Sleeplessness, particularly after eating too late. Fainting fits. Rheumatism with sensation of numbness and lameness of the affected part. Gout. *Ague* of not too long standing; the coldness prevailing during the paroxysms, but not of much violence, though of longer duration than the heat, recuring even in the latter.

SKIN. Measles.

HEAD. Dullness. Giddiness. Heaviness. Tearing, stinging pain.

FACE. Pain, extending into the eye and ear.

EARS. Humming, buzzing, roaring. Hardness of hearing. Shrinking, tearing pain. Painfulness and pain in the whole side of the head. Sensation of something pressing out of the ear. Sensitiveness of the auditory passage. Discharges.

EYES. Slight inflammation, Much secretion of tears and mucous. Pain. Adhering of the eye-lids. Swelling of the eye-lids. Sty.

NOSE. Catarrh, particularly when the appetite is very soon lost. Much secretion of mucous. Impossibility of smelling. Stoppage. Bleeding with violent sneezing.

MOUTH. *Very coated tongue.* Flat or bitter taste. Tearing, drawing toothache; pain in the whole side, extending into the ears.

STOMACH AND BOWELS. Complaints after having taken *fat* food, (pork). Bitter or sour eructations. *Loathing of food, particularly of warm.* Nausea, vomiting, (Ipecac.). Pain in the stomach. Griping colic. Pain with distention and fullness of the abdomen. Sensitiveness to touch. Rumbling. *Diarrhœa.*

URINARY SYSTEM. Difficult, painful passing of water. Painful pressure on the bladder. Too frequent discharge of water. Copious, light-colored urine. Wetting of the bed. Retention of urine. Palsy of the bladder.

SEXUAL SYSTEM. Frequent erections and emissions, sometimes painful. Excited sexual desire. Swelling and painfulness of the testicles. Painful swelling of the back part of the testicles and of the seminal cord. Too tardy appearance of the first terms. *Terms with thin, watery discharge.* Terms with heaviness and painful pressure, like labors. *Terms too scant, too late, too short. Suppressed terms. Greensickness. Labors too weak. Hemorrhage*, caused by laxness or inactivity of the womb during or after child-birth.* Very painful after-pains, following a too quick or easy birth. *Whites*, particularly before and after the terms.

THROAT AND CHEST. Slight hoarseness and soreness, (Bell.). *Loose cough. Very easy*

---

* If the womb is well contracted after delivery, a hard tumor of the size of a goose-egg is felt, in pressing the abdomen gently over the share-bone.

raising of thin, whitish, yellowish *mucous*, (Spitting of black, coagulated blood). Sensation of suffocation, particularly at night. Short breathing. Palpitation of the heart.

RHUS TOXICODENDRON.

GENERAL. *Complaints in consequence of having worn wet cloths. Rheumatism* with tearing, drawing pain, or like that after sprains, with numbness and pricking, worse in rest, better in motion; the affected part swollen, red, and brilliant. Rheumatism of the small of the back. Gout. Very violent fever (in the later stages of diseases,) with weak, intermittent pulse, delirium or stupor, involuntary discharges, etc.

SKIN. Nettle rash. Erysipelas bullosum. Blisters, filled with an acrid fluid. Pustules, particularly on the face. Red tip of the nose or red spots.

HEAD. Giddiness with a sensation, when moving, as if the brain were reverberating or trembling, or as if it were loose. Pain.

EYES. Inflammation with secretion of very acrid tears, causing soreness of the cheek.

MOUTH. Violent drawing, jerking toothache, as if the tooth were being torn out; throbbing and tearing pain in both jaws, extending into the ears and head; worse in the open air or at night, better by external warmth; hollow teeth becoming loosened; the gum swollen. Offensive breath.

BOWELS. Griping colic. Diarrhœa.

LIMBS. Numbness. Sensation of prickling. Easily falling asleep. Palsy, particularly of the arms.

SILICEA.

Particularly to be considered in the following cases:

1. *Affections of the bones*, as pain, ulceration, swelling, rickets, etc.

2. *Festering of long standing* of any part of the body, but particularly when there are *fistules*, (Calc.), or when the festering places do not heal or heal very slowly.

3. *Scrofulous disease*, (Hep., Calc., Sulph., Merc.).

SKIN. Ulcers. Fellon.

FACE. Pain, particularly when in the bones.

EARS. Discharges. Buzzing. Humming. Sensation of stoppage, sometimes ending with a cracking noise. Great sensitiveness of hearing. Hardness of hearing.

NOSE. Stoppage. Swelling and bloating of the mucous membrane. Chronic cold. Ulceration of the bones. Secretion of matter. Scabs and scurf on the nostrils. Polypus. Bleeding.

MOUTH. Toothache, when the pain is seated more in the jaw and adjacent bones, than in the teeth.

SPONGIA MARINA TOSTA.

GENERAL. Goitre.

SEXUAL ORGANS. Hardness, swelling and painfulness of the testicles.

THROAT AND CHEST. Hoarseness. *Painfulness of the throat. Violent, hoarse, rough or barking cough.* Very difficult breathing. Danger of suffocation. Whistling respiration.

SULPHUR.

Particularly to be considered in the following cases:

1. *In diseases of long standing and especially in those of the skin, or when the latter have been forcibly suppressed by improper external treatment; also with persons, who have suffered from* chronic *diseases of the skin.*

2. *In scrofula and consumption,* (tuberculosis).

When a remedy gives only temporary relief, it proves frequently successful to give it in alternation with *Sulph.*

General. Great sleepiness during daytime, particularly in the afternoon and evening, but sleeplessness at night. *Varicose, dilated veins.* Liability to rheumatism. Gout. Hypochondriasis. Cramp of the calves of the legs. Epilepsy. Palsy.

Skin. *Pimples. Blisters*, filled with acrid fluid. *Pustules. Scabs.* Itching. Ulcers. Boils. Nettle rash. Small pox, measles, scarlet fever, particularly in delay of the eruption. *Itch.*

Head. Dullness, giddiness, pain.

Ears. Buzzing, humming. Hardness of hearing. Mattery discharges.

Eyes. Chronic inflammation, (Merc., Hep.).

Nose. Chronic cold, (Hep., Calc.). Swelling. Liability to bleed very easily.

Mouth. Swollen upper lip. Bad, fetid taste. Coated tongue.

Stomach and bowels. Want of appetite. Eructations. Heartburn. Nausea. Loathing of food. Waterbrash. Pressure in the stomach after any kind of food. Weak digestion. Distention of the abdomen. Griping colic. Emissions of fetid smelling wind. *Costiveness.** Frequent but unsuccessful desire to evacuate. *Chronic, painless diarrhœa** or *liability to it.* Acrid discharges with soreness of the anus, (Merc.). *Piles.* Itching of the piles. Rupture. Worms, causing periodical itching in the anus. Liability to worms.

Urinary organs. Painful, difficult passing of water. Wetting of the bed.

Sexual organs. Emissions. Terms too late, too scant, too short. Suppression of the terms. Greensickness. Terms too soon, too long, too copious. *Whites* with secretion of acrid mucous, (Merc.).

Throat and chest. (Chronic) hoarseness with weak, husky voice. Exhausting cough with thick, mattery expectoration during daytime. Bloody expectoration. Much loose mucous in the ramifications of the wind-pipe, (Tart. emet.). Pain and soreness in the chest. Very difficult breathing, forcing the patient to sit up, particularly at night, with or without dry cough. Palpitation of the heart.

---

* Frequently, when *costiveness* prevails, this remedy is successfully given in alternation with *Nux*, when *diarrhœa*, with *China*.—*Sulph.* in the morning, *Nux* or *Chin.* in the evening.

Tartarus emeticus.

General. Somnolency. *Rheumatism of the joints*, which are painful, swollen and red.

Tongue, stomach and bowels. Coated tongue. Flat, bad taste. Fetid eructations. Rising of food or sour, sharp fluids. *Nausea. Retching, vomiting*, (Ipecac.). Pain and distention of the abdomen. Diarrhœa.

Nose, throat and chest. *Scabs or scurf in the nose* or *on the nostrils.* (Chronic) catarrh of the nose or in the head, *when there is a constant secretion of a little mucous in the back part of the nose, near the palate, which causes the patient to "hawk" often.* Soreness of the throat. *Much loose mucous in the throat and wind-pipe*, causing rattling, with or without cough. *Much loose cough*, (Puls.). Foamy or watery expectoration. (Very) difficult, short breathing and pressure in the chest, *relieved by raising mucous.* Asthma. *Danger of suffocation* in consequence of much foamy phlegm in the ramifications of the wind-pipe. Pain and soreness in the chest.

Veratrum album.

General. *Great agitation. Despair. Inconsolable despondency. Fear of death. Cold perspiration. Chills. Cold limbs. General coldness. Great weakness, debility. Exhaustion. Prostration, Asphyxy. Slow, weak pulse.* Fainting fits. Malignant, cholera-like cases of *ague ;* the paroxysms distinguished by prevailing coldness and slight heat followed by great weakness.

HEAD. Giddiness, pain.

FACE. *Pale, haggared, hollow-cheeked face. Bluish, cadaverous complexion.* Blue circles around the eyes.

EYES. Squinting.

MOUTH. Cold tongue. Thirst, (Ars.).

STOMACH AND BOWELS. *Nausea. Frequent vomiting. Griping colic. Frequent watery discharges.*

CHEST. *Violent cough*, causing retching and vomiting. Very difficult and short breathing. Asthma. Cold breath. Palpitation of the heart..

LIMBS. *Cramps of the calves of the legs.* Palsy of the legs.